Praise for *The Legend Liminal*

"*The Legend Liminal* traps its readers in time and space, where we, like the characters, are moving forward yet stuck in place—a melancholic meditation on grief and the inability to move on; of finding the purpose and meaning of existence; of travelling without knowing the destination." —**Ai Jiang, Nebula and Bram Stoker and Hugo Award finalist and author of *A Palace Near the Wind* and *Linghun***

"This mind-trip of a book well captures the expansive freedom of road trips, combined with the emotional complexity of longstanding relationships, both friend and familial. The story puts the reader into a liminal space - one that is just familiar enough to feel grounded, but odd enough to keep you asking 'wtf is happening' in the best way." —**Khan Wong, author of *The Circus Infinite* and *Down in the Sea of Angels***

"As imaginative and nostalgic as *Stranger Things*, mixed with the twisty conundrum of *Groundhog Day*, *The Legend Liminal* is a fresh, clever, and sometimes creepy road trip—don't miss hitching a ride!" —**Kate Murray, author of *We Who Hunt the Hollow***

"*The Legend Liminal* is an ambitiously original novella about the strength of familial bonds in all the strangest, coldest corners of spacetime, and the subtle defiance of simply existing in an uncertain world. Hutchings' signature wit and twisty sci-fi concepts add kaleidoscopic depth to this standout story." —**Claire Winn, author of *City of Shattered Light***

"Anyone who's ever felt trapped in their worst moments will find resonance in this evocative slipstream story of empty spaces, endless highways, and the people who give the world meaning when there's nothing else left." —**Rebecca Fraimow, author of Locus Award finalist *Lady Eve's Last Con***

THE LEGEND LIMINAL

REN HUTCHINGS

ISBN: 979-8-9914419-5-7 (trade paper)
ISBN: 979-8-9914419-6-4 (ePub)
Library of Congress Catalog Number: 2025939310

First printing edition: September 30, 2025
Published by Stars and Sabers Publishing in the United States of America.
Cover Artwork: Kim Herbst | Cover Design and Layout: Dash Creative
Edited by Jendia Gammon and Gareth L. Powell
Proofreading and Interior Layout by Scarlett R. Algee

https://www.starsandsabers.com/

For the lost, and the wayfinders, and the still-traveling.

THE
LEGEND
LIMINAL

I like lime slushies and red licorice, lazy summer evenings and walking on sand barefoot. I like glowsticks and the smell of sunscreen, drinking on patios and baking. I like parrots and butterflies and small dogs that wear rain jackets. I like 80s rock music, open-world video games and long sci-fi novels.

My name is Stacey M. Kells, and I exist.

I think I've started narrating the events of my own life in my head to convince myself that I'm still real. I repeat the facts of my existence and comb over them, checking for consistency, probing my memories to make sure they're still there. I lie on my bed in the back of the camper and mentally list out my strengths, weaknesses, and the key events of my back story like I'm making myself a character sheet.

Sometimes I pretend I'm on a reality show, and we're just about to be told we got punked. It's wishful thinking, of course, but it's comforting to imagine that *someone* is still watching us. Even if they're making fun of us. Even if I'm not anybody's favorite contestant. Even if I'm never going to be the most interesting character in the story.

I don't really think anyone *is* watching us anymore, if they ever were. The truth is, there's nobody else here. A few days ago, the world got real empty, and it's stayed empty. Or maybe everyone else is still out there living their normal lives, and the world never changed—because it's just the four of us who changed, the four of us who somehow... *slid out of the world.* But regardless of what happened, as far as we can tell, only the four of us exist here. Wherever *here* is.

Now it's just my two brothers, their best friend, and me. Just us, and a map that doesn't make sense anymore, and our sweet, self-sufficient camper. And miles upon miles of desert and sky and endless empty highway.

None of us intended to fall out of reality when we packed our bags, loaded up the van my brothers had been renovating all spring, and started driving west from our hometown. Yeah, sure, we might have *said* something like that—I mean, that's kind of the point of going off the grid, isn't it? Leaving all the shit in your normal life behind for a while, and all that? But no one could have expected it to happen quite so literally. It's been six days since it happened, and part of me still thinks I'm going to wake up from a dream.

I sit on my cot in the back of the camper, wide awake, staring at the same page of my book that I've been on for an hour. Faye is asleep in the identical cot across from me, one leg splayed outside of her blanket, her left arm angled up dramatically over her head. Her electric blue hair is fanned artfully over the pillow, like she's just pretending to sleep while posing for an artsy Instagram shot. Guess it's too bad there's no internet now, and maybe there never will be again. She looks kind of delicate when she sleeps, like a pale spooky angel, but she would probably kill me if I ever said anything like that to her.

Faye Weatherby has been best friends with my brothers ever since they were in junior high. It's always been the three of them: the indestructible, eternal trio. Faye went to a different school, but she met the boys through their mutual friend Marky-O, this hilarious stoner buddy of theirs who's always thrown the best parties. Faye's a gothy tattoo artist with a million piercings, amazing makeup, and the weirdest playlists, and she's always been *way* too cool for both of my brothers—I really have no idea why she started hanging out with them back then.

I used to wonder if either of my brothers ever had a crush on Faye, but I've long since abandoned that notion. Spencer has always been a bit too much of a jock to be Faye's type, and Shelton has never given one single fuck about dating. Faye mostly goes for girls, anyway, and she's only dated the occasional dude. At this point, she's become part of our family, and I'm pretty sure Shel and Spence see her like another sister. The honorary fourth Kells sibling. Honestly, Faye's kind of a stone-cold bitch, but I love her because my brothers love her, and I've never been more glad that she's here.

I stare at the neon digits blinking on the wall clock that's mounted above Faye's cot. Does it still make sense to look at clocks when time is meaningless now? There's some comfort in the numbers, I suppose, in watching them move and change in the way that nothing else really does anymore. (It's 2:22 am now. *Click.* And now it's 2:23.) I imagine that I can hear the minute tick over when the digital display flips, even though all I can actually hear is Faye's faint snoring.

We've been driving across this desert for six days since we last saw another living soul, since that night when we stood outside a gas station counting out change from the cupholder and bickering in front of a broken vending machine. It was such a non-event, that argument, but we've all gone over and over what we said, what we did, where we went after that, a hundred times. That was the last thing that happened before we piled back into the camper, drove out of the parking lot, turned left back onto the highway exit... and fell out of reality.

Shelton is absolutely obsessed with the stop we made at that gas station. He's convinced something happened back at that place—Legend Roadstop—that made us... *cross over*. But Spence thinks it was just a gas station like any other, and it just happened to be the last place we stopped before *the thing* happened to us. He says that gas station means about as much to the outcome as it would if we'd been t-boned by a truck as we pulled back onto the highway. Maybe it's just a place we stopped, like everything else in life.

Not everything means something, Stacey.

Sometimes I wish I had *enjoyed the moment* more, or something. What would I have done if I'd known that standing in that parking lot would be the last moment I'd ever spend in the real world? If I could have held on to the edge of that old reality like a movie protagonist hanging from a cliff, would I have clung to it somehow, clawed my way back, held on for dear life? Or was there something inside me that *wanted* to disappear from the world? Sometimes, I think I would swiftly have uncurled my fingers, released my grip, and let myself slide into this nothing-world anyway.

But it doesn't matter, because there was no way to hang on. There was no warning, no missed chance to turn back. I know deep down that this is just the kind of bullshit we tell ourselves in retrospect—that we could have changed something, that a different choice would have made a difference. We create stories to search for the signs we should've seen, even when there were none there.

I still have the quarter that fell out of that broken vending machine when Faye kicked it. Every day, I put that quarter back into my pocket, and I'm not entirely sure why. At this point, it's like some kind of weird superstition. The quarter looks shiny and new, like maybe no one else has ever touched it before me. For all I know, no one ever did.

But sometimes, a vending machine is just a vending machine, and a gas station is just a gas station. *Not everything means something.*

I stare at the same page in my book until my eyes flutter closed.

) ● (

I'm standing in the gas station bathroom, washing my hands. It's one of those places with a flimsy, graffitied metal door that opens straight to outside, where you have to get the key from behind the counter in the convenience store before you can use it. Inside, it smells mostly like pee, with a faint veneer of some floral-scented cleaning product over the top—like someone gave it a spritz of air freshener and called it done.

I examine my face in the cracked mirror, lathering my fingers with that cheap pink soap as I stare at my reflection. Medium-length medium-brown hair that hasn't been washed in a little too long. Medium-sized nose that leans a little to one side, just like Mom's did. Medium-beige skin tone, my cheeks washed out and blueish under the flickering fluorescent bulb. I don't mind how I look, but sometimes I feel like I'm the plainest person who ever lived. I'm just so *bored* of myself.

I push open the bathroom door, tucking the plastic keyring into my jeans pocket, and I walk back out into the parking lot. The moon is high in the sky: one of those freakishly large and pretty full moons that makes you want to take a picture of it. Our camper is parked in one of the gas pump bays, off to my left. In front of me are my brothers and Faye, standing beside that broken vending machine, bickering about who's going to drive when we get back in the van. I start walking toward them. This time, I wake up before I see Faye kick the machine, but I already know that's what's going to happen, because the same thing always does.

Before the nothing-world, I almost never used to have dreams about things that happened in real life—at least, not hyperrealistic play-by-play re-enactments of them, where I just relive the same pointless conversation over and over. But maybe dreaming in a nothing-world has separate rules. Maybe we lose our capacity to dream about anything new here, because new things don't exist anymore.

Seriously, who has a dream about *standing in a gas station bathroom?* This is exactly why I'm sure that if this *is* some kind of reality show, I'm the team member no one ever remembers. And if there does end up being a serial killer or a zombie attack or something, I'm definitely not surviving to the last act.

) ● (

When I open my eyes again, the book I was not-reading is on the floor, and I'm smushed uncomfortably against the compartment wall with my reading glasses still on. I shove them back into their case and throw them into my backpack as I sit up. It's past four in the morning now.

I get up and stretch, then peer through our beaded curtain into Shelton's compartment. The receipt from that damned roadstop is still pinned to the bulletin board on the wall above Shel's desk, in the middle of a sea of notes and Polaroid photos and maps he's tacked up in there. All he needs is some red string and it'd look just like that one meme with the unhinged-looking guy and the corkboard. If Shel as a person had to be summed up as a meme, that'd probably be it, so it's fitting that he's actually re-created it in here.

Shel's "office" takes up most of the middle segment of the camper, right across from our tiny kitchenette and the cubby where we keep our plastic plates and our coffee mugs. Instead of a bed, he installed a desk in there that takes up the same footprint as a cot would've—which is pretty much a classic Shel decision. He sleeps in an old nylon sleeping bag that's crammed halfway under the desk. I guess it's still marginally better than Spence's situation, 'cause Spence sleeps across the front seat bench, in the same place he sits most of the day when he's driving. Somehow, Spence is always the one who gets the roughest deal, and we don't appreciate him nearly enough for it.

But now, peering through the curtain, I'm surprised to see that Shel isn't at his desk, *or* underneath it. His sleeping bag is empty, and so is his chair. The papers he was working on are still there; a bunch of notes and hand-drawn maps are scattered around the desk alongside like a dozen empty energy drink cans. His laptop's gone, though, and that's weird. He goes out for a smoke at night sometimes, but never with his laptop.

"Shel? Hey, Shel, you out there?" I call out the half-open window.

My neck prickles with certainty that something's wrong, and even as the thought crosses my mind, I can't help but laugh to myself. Of course something's fucking *wrong*. Nothing's been right since we left that gas station and drove out into the desert. Since the map changed. Since we've been...here. I shove all those thoughts away, packaging them neatly into a back drawer in my mind as I push open the side door of the camper.

Shel is standing just outside the door, looking up at the sky. He's got his laptop out there, set up on top of one of our folding tables, and he's squinting up at the stars, then scribbling something down on the notebook in his hand. He mutters to himself, ignoring me completely.

"Shel? Hey... Shel?"

He finally whips around to face me. "What, Stace, *what?!*"

"Wow, okay, chill. I was just coming to see what you're doing out here." I kick at the metal step that hangs below the door. "I noticed your laptop was gone, and... I wanted to check if you were okay."

My brother's face softens then, and he reaches out to put a hand on my shoulder. "Shit. I'm sorry, Stace. Really. I... I didn't mean for it to come out that way."

Shelton is definitely the more reserved of my two brothers. He doesn't go into protector-mode on me like Spencer, but he does care, and occasionally he even tries to show it. He's what Faye calls 'emotionally constipated,' which is kind of funny because Faye is one hundred percent the type of person who runs away screaming if you imply she might be having a feeling. I guess Spence and I are the softies that balance them out.

Spence and Shel were born less than a year apart, and they've always been stuck together. They were in the same grade at school, they have all the same friends, and they couldn't even pick separate besties. I'm almost exactly four years younger than Shel; young enough for my brothers to call me 'kiddo' growing up, but not quite so much of a baby that I could never hang out with their friend group. My brothers were pains in the ass when we were kids, but they've never excluded me from anything. And, especially after Mom died, the three of us have always had each other's backs.

"So... are you going to explain what you're up to out here or what, Professor McWeirdass?" I say to Shel. I poke his shoulder teasingly, but he doesn't smile.

He gestures at the laptop, then back up at the sky. "*I wish* I could explain this to you, Stacey. Honestly...I'm seeing some pretty strange stuff right now. See that, up there?"

He points up into the sky, and I follow his gaze. There's nothing much to see, just a bunch of stars and the occasional wispy cloud. It's a perfect night for stargazing.

"No, not really. I don't see anything."

"*Exactly!*" His eyes go wide, like he's expecting me to have had some kind of revelation. He pushes his chunky black glasses up, even though they're already about as high up his nose as they can get. It's a nervous habit he has, that glasses-pushing thing, and he's been doing it a lot lately. "Do you remember when we stopped at the gas station, Stace? When we were out by that vending machine trying to count the change?"

"Yeah. We've only talked about it eight billion times, dude." I give an exaggerated sigh. I never want to talk about that vending machine again in my life.

"Right, well... do you remember the sky that night?" He gestures up again. "There was a full moon that night, Stace. *Full. Moon.*" He looks at me, waiting for his words to sink in. "How long ago was that?"

"Six days." Not like we haven't talked about *that* eight billion times either.

"Exactly. Which means we should definitely be seeing a waning moon up there tonight!" He shakes his head. "But we're not. No. Look, there's no moon up there at all."

I squint into the sky. "What, so...are you saying the moon's *disappeared* or something?"

He rolls his eyes at me, as if what I said is any more outrageous than anything else that's happened to us already. "No, Stace. I'm saying it looks like it's been a lot more than a week since then. I'm saying... *time's acting weird.*"

I stare at him. "A lot more than a week? Since we were at that gas station?"

He nods solemnly. "Yeah."

"But...that's impossible! I'm still eating that same box of cereal—"

He raises his hands defensively. "I don't know what to tell you. This shit's freakin' me out, Stace." He fixes me with a piercing gaze. "But what I *think* about it doesn't matter, does it? Look at the sky. Something *happened.* We aren't where we're supposed to be anymore."

The next morning, I wake to find Faye and Shel standing outside the camper talking. Shel can be real intense sometimes, and Faye has an incredibly bitchy morning voice, so I'm not entirely sure if they're just chatting or if they're arguing. But I can hear them through the window while I'm making my coffee, talking in tense voices just slightly too quietly for me to make out the words.

Spence has clearly already removed himself from this conversation. He's sitting on a lawn chair out by the fire pit we dug yesterday, pretending he's not listening to them. He stares into the middle distance, idly scuffing one toe around the cold, charred remnants of last night's campfire, swilling coffee out of a travel mug.

I just saw Spence's dirty mug on the counter, and he's totally using Faye's instead of washing out his own— which I'm *sure* would have prompted some kind of drama, except for the fact that Shel got to her first. I think Shel's probably in the middle of explaining his 'time is acting weird' hypothesis, telling her about the moon changing, and she isn't taking it well.

As I head outside, I bang open the camper door in the way that's sure to wind Spence up. I don't know why I do it, but I think lightly annoying at least one of my brothers before breakfast has become a kind of grounding ritual for me. A way to remind myself that some things are still normal.

"Stacey, c'mon!" Spence shouts from the fire pit. "I've told you a thousand times not to whip the door like that when you open it."

Bingo. I let my mouth quirk up into a sarcastic smile. Guess we're still real after all. I don't apologize for whipping the door. In fact, I slam it extra hard as I close it behind me, watching Spence cringe and roll his eyes at me, and I only feel a little bit guilty.

Spence has never quite stopped treating me like a child. Ever since he signed those papers to take legal responsibility for me when Mom died—when he was twenty and I was fifteen—he's always been protective. And he's never stopped telling me what to do, despite the fact that I'm the same age now as he was when he became my guardian. I don't think it really matters how many times I remind him that I'm a whole goddamn adult now, I'll always be 'kiddo' to him.

But deep down, I know I can never really repay Spence for doing what he did for us. He was supposed to be going to university that fall. He'd already spent two years saving for it, and he'd been accepted to a decent school in the city. Instead, he stayed in our boring hometown so I could finish high school. He went to work full-time for the construction company, and he used up his entire savings fund paying down Mom's debts.

I guess Spence is never going to university now. Pretty sure there's no such thing as a degree anymore in nothing-world, anyway.

"Material evidence! We have it!" Shel is saying to Faye. "There's proof of when we were at that roadstop. The evidence is still here." He holds up that creased receipt like it's some kind of holy relic. "Here's our receipt from the gas station. Look. This is exactly what you remember buying, right? Energy drinks, a case of water, two bags of Doritos, a box of cereal. We all agree this is what happened, right?" He flaps the receipt in her face. "Legend Roadstop. June 14th, 10:52 pm. $40.00 cash. $1.35 back in change."

"Okay, yeah, I get it! The goddamn receipt, fine! But what's your *point*?" Faye heaves a sigh. "It was June 14th when we bought that stuff, but now your moon phase calendar says more time passed than we think. Fine. That is absolutely batshit-bonkers, Shelton, what do you want me to say? Even if it's true, what the hell are we supposed to do with that information?"

Beside the fire pit, Spence is peering over the top of his sunglasses, very obviously eavesdropping. He might as well be in some kind of detective cartoon for how obvious he's being. Faye glances over there and her eyes land on her shiny black travel mug clutched in his hands. Her mouth tenses in that way it does right before she loses her shit.

"Spence, are you listening to this?" she says. "Did you hear about all of Shelton's '*time is acting weird*' stuff?"

"Yeah. I heard." Spence shrugs with what looks like genuine

indifference. "But also..." He pauses dramatically and gestures around. "We could consider the fact that... there is literally *nobody else left on the planet* right now? That feels like a *way* bigger problem than what is or isn't in the sky. I can't say I'm really that bothered about the moon calendar."

"Nonetheless, we need to gather information," Shel says, his voice rising in frustration. "There's an answer here somewhere. We just need to apply ourselves to the problem!"

Faye stalks over to Spence and snatches her mug out of his hands. "Yeah, okay. And Spence needs to *apply himself* to rinsing out his own coffee mug. Gimme that, thank you very much."

I kneel down by the fire pit and pick up a stick. I flick it around in my hands, tracing aimless patterns in last night's ashes, trying not to think too hard.

Sometimes it feels like maybe the whole universe burned down, and we're here just driving around in the little pile of what's left.

Around midday, we pull off the highway at another roadstop to pick up some more food. There's a couple of picnic tables on the lawn out front, and a big empty parking lot with no cars in it. Parked around the back of the building on a patch of grass, there's a rusty old pickup that looks like it would barely run. Shel wants Spence to come with him to check the truck out anyway, because he has to search every single car we find to see if there's anything personal in it. There never is. The cars are always unlocked, no keys, no stuff. Shel records the make and model in his notebook.

"Think about it—a normal car would always have *some* stuff in it, right?" Shel is saying. "Like, you'd always have your sunglasses or a parking pass or something in there, or a junk flyer you didn't throw out, or at least a license and registration in the glove box. Right? But none of the cars we find have *anything* in them."

"I don't like it," Faye says, making a face. "Hmm... but wouldn't it be even creepier if random people's stuff *was* still in there? Or if there was, like, a bag of still-warm fast food just sitting on the front seat or something?"

"Ugh. Congrats, you officially found a way to make it creepier," Spence says, laughing and wincing at the same time. "Thanks, Faye."

"No problem." She gives him a mock salute, and almost cracks a smile for the first time all day. "Glad to be of service."

I go to grab our supply baskets from the van—that is to say, the two scuffed milk crates that we use to carry shit in. Faye and I head for the store to stock up on food, while Shel and Spence go to look at that damn truck. I push open the glass door, and a chime jingles uselessly overhead. There's no one coming to ring us up. Of course there's no one in here at all.

I look around. Whatever else is wrong and missing in this nothing-world, it seems like the electricity grid is still up, because the store is fully lit and powered, fluorescent lights and fridges and all. The register still looks functional, and the lotto machine is blinking away behind the counter, flashing an ad with pixelated coins falling down, a tinny voice chanting *winner, winner, winner* every thirty seconds.

Aside from the fact that there's nobody in it, it looks like a boring-ass regular roadside convenience store, with the usual selection of canned stuff and candy and snacks. Per Shel's instructions, I make sure I look around to see if I can find a date on anything, but as usual, there's nothing here. No newspapers or magazines, and no sign of anything that would change with the passage of time. None of the food has expiry dates printed on it.

I grab a jumbo caramel chocolate bar from the nearest rack and walk behind the counter to ring myself up, just for shits and giggles. I scan the bar with the wand—$2.78—and I type in a tender of five dollars cash.

Change due: $2.22. The cash register bangs open.

The drawer is totally empty, of course. I fish my cracked blue wallet out of my bag, take out a five-dollar bill and lay it delicately into the empty register, like it's some kind of reverent offering. I stare down at it, that worn, creased bit of paper money from the real world, and I'm suddenly on the verge of tears. It looks so *normal*, and yet everything about this is so… *not.*

I can't make any change, but it hardly matters.

I close the drawer, and the machine dutifully prints me a receipt, the familiar whine and buzz of the printer incongruously jarring in the silence. I tear the paper off and look at it. The ink seems to be running out; my receipt is just a blur of faint grey horizontal lines. Huh. I fold it and slide it into the side pocket of my wallet—Shel will probably want to study it later.

When I look up, Faye is coming back toward me, carrying an already-overflowing basket of supplies. Half of her milk crate is full of small bottles of Dr Pepper, like she cleaned the whole shelf out. I look at her and roll my eyes. She must've taken every single Dr Pepper they had.

"Hey! What the hell are you doing back there, Stacey?" she yells. "C'mon. Fill up your basket, let's load up so we can get out of here. I hate going in these places."

I walk out from behind the register, leaving the chocolate bar I just paid for on the counter—I don't even like caramel chocolate. I go over to the nearest shelf and shovel a bunch of stuff into my crate without really looking at it. Instant potatoes, coffee for the coffee maker, a few cans of soup and vegetables, a big can of ready-made stew. I fill up the rest of the crate with a couple more bags of Doritos for Spence. There. That'll do. It hardly matters what I get; we can always pull over again and get more stuff at the next stop.

"Okay, I'm done. Let's go."

Faye doesn't wait for me. She bolts right out the door and back toward the camper with her basket practically before the words have left my mouth.

I pause as I reach the door, and I look back at the flashing lotto machine and the closed register. I think of my five-dollar bill sitting in there like some sort of time capsule, and I wonder if anyone will ever lay eyes on it again. Maybe some future archaeologists will find it in there, and use it as definitive proof that somebody was still alive out here after the... whatever-it-was that happened.

If there *is* a future. If there *are* still archaeologists to find it.

I shudder and look away again. I heft the milk crate under the crook of one arm, pull open the door, and follow Faye out into the parking lot.

Back at the camper, I take the misprinted receipt out of my wallet and I place it on Shel's desk.

I stare down at the wallet in my hands, the same grungy blue vinyl foldout that I've had since the summer Mom died. I've meant to get a new one for a long time, but I guess I just never quite got around to it, like so many other things. Now, I run my nails along those familiar greying cracks while all of reality is cracking apart.

I turn it over and over in my hands, open and close it, fold it and unfold it. I flip through my ID, my bank cards and loyalty cards over and over, like I'm expecting something to have changed. Like I might pull out my driver's license only to find it's a blank piece of plastic, because Stacey Melian Kells never existed at all.

Stacey Melian Kells. Mom was a massive Tolkien nerd; that's why we all have the middle names we do. I don't know if I find it funnier that Shel has to sign all his legal stuff with *Shelton Aragorn Kells*, or that Spence's middle name is literally just *John*. I like my own name just fine, but I never really cared about it one way or another before Mom died. After that, it meant something different to me.

Mom named me Stacey after the taxi driver who took her to the hospital when her water broke halfway through her shift at the coffee shop. Stacey picked Mom up even though she was just coming in for her coffee break, and she didn't turn on the fare meter. Mom said it reminded her that there are still small kindnesses in the world, and she wanted that to be the one thing I would never forget.

I know I could throw my ID cards out the window of the camper and just name myself anything I want now. In this nothing-world, I could be Not-Stacey. There's something tempting about that, and this empty world echoes with anonymity. Who's ever going to know? But here, in the middle of all this nothingness, I cling to my name more than I ever have. I'm compelled to write it down, and I write it over and over again. It's as if this particular sequence of letters anchors me to the *before*, to where I came from, to what I was—to what I could have been.

I take the receipt back from Shel's desk and I keep it instead. I take out my black Sharpie and I write on the back: *Stacey M. Kells ~~was~~ is here. Stacey M. Kells is alive. Stacey M. Kells is real.* Then I slide it back into my wallet, and put my wallet back into my bag.

) ● (

When I exit the camper, the boys have returned from checking out the truck, and now they're hanging out with Faye over by the picnic tables. I'm guessing they didn't find anything interesting in there, because they all look bored as hell.

"Maybe this is all a dream," Spence is saying. He's spinning the keys to the camper round and round in his hand like a fidget toy. "I mean, yeah, it's a totally elaborate one that feels freakishly real but… we *could* be dreaming, right? Or maybe it's like… a bad trip? We did do a *lot* of mushrooms that weekend before we left, when Marky-O came over."

"Sure," says Shel. "If you want." He's obviously not listening. He's sitting on top of one of the picnic tables with his nose stuck in a tattered notebook that's got tons of papers and notes shoved into it.

"I didn't do any mushrooms when Marky-O came over," I point out. "So why am *I* here?"

Faye scoffs like she's clearing her throat. "Yeeeeah. I dunno. I've had some bad trips in my life, but nothin' like this." She's lying down across the opposite picnic table, her shiny black Doc Martens hanging down onto the bench. She's holding her phone in her hand, slowly waving it back and forth over her head, still trying to find a signal. I've long ago given up trying.

"You find a network yet, Faye?" Spence asks.

Faye turns her head and gives him a withering glare. "Yeah, sure I did, dingus. I've actually been livestreaming on Instagram for the last hour and I just forgot to tell you about it."

"Okay, wow, damn. You don't have to jump down my throat like that all the time." For a second, my brother looks genuinely hurt. He shoves the camper key back into his pocket, then stalks off alone, moving further down the parking lot. All of our tempers are rapidly fraying, and it's only going to get worse from here if we don't try to chill the fuck out.

I run my hand over the weathered surface of the picnic table Shel is sitting on. There's the usual graffiti on it—a couple of band names, a gouged-out heart with an arrow through it, and a barely-legible old scrawl that says *JB wuz here.*

I dig my black Sharpie out of my backpack again and I write on an empty board on the table:

We were here. We ARE here. We are alive.
Stacey M. Kells
Shelton A. Kells
Spencer J. Kells
Faye

I pause and glance at Faye. She's finally put her phone down on her chest and she's lying there with her eyes closed. Something about her expression makes me think she's about to cry, and I hope to hell she isn't. I don't think I could cope anymore if Faye broke down, if she started sobbing and sniffling instead of just being snarky and pissed off.

"You got a middle name, Faye?" In all these years, I don't think I've ever asked her.

"Yeah, I do. It's 'Go Eat Butts, Stacey.' Don't know what my parents were thinking."

I roll my eyes. "Thanks."

I write: *Faye Weatherby is still a jerk. That's how I know this is real.*

I feel a little bit bad for writing on that table that Faye is a jerk. But it's not my fault that it seems like exactly the kind of eternal fact that would be true in every version of reality. Faye *is* a jerk. In fact, she's a total asshole most of the time, but she's the honorary Kells sibling, and she's one of us. She's been friends with my brothers for more than thirteen years, and she's the closest thing to a sister that I'll ever have. She's here with us just like she should be, and I wouldn't want it any other way.

The three of them bicker every damn day, but there has only ever been one time when Faye and my brothers had anything like a real falling-out. I'll never forget it—the worst summer of my life, the summer Mom died. The closest I've come to feeling like my whole world was disappearing before now, before it actually did.

It started with a party that we never should have gone to. A month after Mom died, Marky-O invited us all to a kegger at his place, and for some godforsaken reason the boys and I decided that we would go.

Spencer had just retracted his university acceptance and signed the papers to become my legal guardian, and he was in the darkest place I've ever seen him. Shelton was always angry, listening to screamo music at wall-shaking volume for hours while not talking to us and getting high in his room all day. Me, I was just trying to get through the summer, lying in bed until two or three in the afternoon, playing video games and streaming reality TV while crying.

Yeah, we were *totally* ready to go have pretend fun at a party. I have no idea why we didn't see what was coming. Unsurprisingly, the night of the party was a complete disaster for all of us—so awful, in fact, that it was immortalized in our Kells vernacular as The Shitshow Saturday.

It was the middle of July, a night so humid and sticky that I felt like I couldn't breathe. There were a ton of people at Marky-O's house, in the backyard and in the pool and in the kitchen and in the basement—people *everywhere*, and I started freaking out almost the minute we got there. I half-considered calling Faye right away to pick me up. Faye wasn't at that party, for some reason I can't remember, but she was standing by to DD us home whenever we called her. We all knew Spence and Shel were planning to get absolutely hammered.

I didn't drink, but in my immense fifteen-year-old wisdom, I decided the best thing to do that night to distract myself would be to get to second base in a closet with my on-again off-again boyfriend Ian—who also happened to be Marky-O's cousin. I hadn't seen Ian since he awkwardly hugged me goodbye after Mom's funeral. I don't think he really knew what to say to me when he saw me at the party, so we just started making out instead of talking.

The whole endeavor went about as well as you'd expect. That is to say, I totally killed the mood when I started sobbing before he'd even unhooked my bra. Ian was a dick about it and took it personally, we had a huge fight, and about an hour later we proceeded to break up dramatically in front of like twenty people in Marky-O's crammed kitchen.

After Ian left and went home, I ended up crying my eyes out on the patio steps. Spence found me out there and sat with me, patting my back and making futile attempts to comfort me—forever determined to be the reliable big bro, despite being so drunk he could hardly string a sentence together. He had to get up twice to go puke in the bushes, and he kept apologizing to me for not being better at looking after me—at least, that's what I thought he was saying. I could barely understand him.

And then, Spence started crying too, and we sat there looking like a goddamn sad, pathetic pair of losers. In the background, people were still dancing and drinking and jumping in the pool and having *real* fun, which only served to rub it in. I remember that somebody was blasting that ridiculous "Cat Said Meow" song on loop, over and over again on the pool speakers, and I thought I was going to lose my mind.

Spence called Faye like a dozen fucking times, but she didn't pick up her phone. We tried to call Shel to tell him we were walking home, but he didn't answer either—turns out he'd dropped his phone in the pool before he went inside to play drinking games, and then he passed out in Marky-O's TV room in the basement. We walked around the party for a while looking for him, but we couldn't find him, so eventually we just left.

It took Spence and I more than two hours to get to our front door, at which point Spence realized that Shel was the only one who had taken house keys. We were locked out of the house. That was the point when we both started crying again.

We were still sitting on the porch, my big brother and I both bawling like babies, when Faye drove up to our house at four in the morning and dropped Shelton off. I guess she finally went to look for us at the party when she saw all our missed calls, and she found Shel— who by then was sobering up and furious with us for leaving without him.

"What a fucking shitshow," was all Shel said to us as he stormed up to the porch. He walked right past us, unlocked the front door, went inside, and slammed it behind him. Faye had already driven away the second Shel got out of her car. It was a whole mess.

In the weeks right after The Shitshow Saturday, there was a strange energy in the group. Spence was still pissed at Faye for not picking up her phone that night, and at Shel for how he acted when he got home. Shel was pissed at Spence for leaving the party without telling him, and at Faye for some argument they had in the car when she drove him home. My brothers were barely speaking to each other *or* Faye, and she didn't come over to our house for weeks.

I tried and tried to talk to my brothers, to somehow pull them back together. I posted memes that I knew Faye would find funny in our four-person *Kells Krew* group chat, but they all went unanswered. It felt like everything was on the brink of falling apart, and the thought of the eternal trio shattering permanently was terrifying. I couldn't handle the thought of anything else in our lives disintegrating. I was so desperate not to lose anyone else.

In time, the events of that cursed party faded into memory, and my brothers *finally* stopped giving each other the cold shoulder. Faye started hanging out at our house like before, and after a while longer, the trio felt solid and eternal again. It was like none of it ever happened.

In time, I did get to second base with a different guy, one who didn't get mad at me or act like a dick, on a night when I didn't cry at all. But the remaining weeks of that summer felt like the longest of my life. And I still *hate* that "Cat Said Meow" song.

I'm lying on my cot in the camper reading, and we're driving west on the highway—well, Spence is driving again, because he basically *never* lets anyone else do it. I feel the vehicle rolling to a slow stop, like we're pulling over, so I set down my book and sit up, wondering if we're going to start moving again. But a good minute later, the camper is still idling on the side of the road.

"Hey, Stace... why'd we stop here?" Faye peers out the window, then looks over at me quizzically from across the compartment, as if I have any more clue than she does.

I shrug, folding up my reading glasses. "No idea, dude."

We both get up curiously and make our way into Shel's office in the middle compartment, but he's already all the way up front, leaning over the seat bench and talking to Spence.

Shel turns around and motions us closer. "C'mon! Check this out," he whispers urgently. God knows why he's *whispering*, but my skin is immediately crawling with dread.

I look outside, prepared for just about anything. There could be a fucking spaceship full of aliens out there and I don't know if I'd really be surprised—I'd probably just be relieved to see another living creature, to be honest. But all I can see is a highway exit. There's just a regular green-and-white lettered sign like all the others, reading *EXIT 151.*

And then, I look a little higher up, and I see what my brothers are staring at. It's one of those digital signs over the highway, the kind that usually shows you messages about upcoming traffic or critical news or those highway PSAs like "please wear your damn seatbelt, fools."

The orange letters are scrolling past, round and round on a repeating loop: *EMERGENCY ASSISTANCE REQUESTED AHEAD – EXIT 151.*

"Whoa," Faye says. "So... does that mean... do you think someone else is out here?"

"Who knows?" Shel jabs a finger at his glasses, shoving them up higher on his nose. "I guess it could be automated, and it got set off by whatever did...all of this." He gestures at the totally empty road ahead of us. "But there's a chance somebody set that alert off manually. I think we've got to investigate."

"Look, hang on. Chill out a second," Spence says. "We've got to think about this first. If there's someone else here, and they called for help... we've got to be careful. They're probably gonna be expecting, like, the army or something. Y'know, the authorities! Not a bunch of useless losers in a camper van."

"Tch, speak for yourself," Faye says, but she laughs anyway. One thing I've discovered on this trip is that Faye has a weird laugh she only does when she's scared. It's funny how you can know someone for so long and still be finding out new things about them.

"I wish I still had a drone left. Maybe we could've scoped things out," Shel sighs.

Faye rolls her eyes. "I think we've already established pretty solidly that the drone thing doesn't really work here."

Shel used to have a bunch of these little drones that he brought along for his aerial photography, but they're all gone now, vanished somewhere into the ether. We lost a couple of them on the very first day after we fell out of reality, when we tried to send them off toward the side of the highway. That was one of the first things we tried doing when we were figuring things out about the nothing-world: using Shel's little drones to get a better view of the terrain around us.

It didn't really accomplish anything, because apparently there's nothing much here. Just desert and desert and desert, the occasional little patch of trees, and miles of highway ahead. Everything worked fine when we sent the drones to look out in front of us. But as soon as we sent one over to the *side* of the highway, its signal suddenly dropped.

After we lost the first one, I watched the second one with binoculars, and I saw it disappear *while we were still looking at it*. It was like it literally just glitched out of existence. Shel wanted to hike over there and have a look at the spot where we lost it, but Spence freaked the hell out, told Shel to get in the van, and drove away.

It's weird, Shel usually just does whatever the hell he wants and won't take directions from anyone... but ever since we got to the nothing-world he's been deferring to Spence again like in the old days. Spence has led the Kells family since Mom died, and there's some things Shel will just never challenge him on. On the rare occasions when Spence's face gets real serious and he says *Don't fuck around, Shelton* in that tone that sounds like Mom's, Shel backs right down.

Later on, we tried attaching Spence's phone to the last drone we had left and flying it around to see if it could pick up a phone network. Surprise, it didn't. Well...I guess technically we don't *know* if it did, because the same thing happened. That drone didn't come back either, and that's how we also lost Spence's phone. Faye's right, the whole drone thing was probably never going to work.

"Just take the damn exit, Spence. Let's drive over there and see what we find," Shel says now. "We'll go real slow, and we'll keep our distance until we can see exactly what's up. Deal?"

"Yeah. Yeah, I think you're right," Spence says. "Let's do it. Stacey? Faye?"

I nod without saying anything. Faye just stands with her arms folded and gives a noncommittal shrug.

Then Spence sticks his fist out and does a silly "team fist-bump" kind of thing with Shel, and this is definitely not something we usually do. But who knows, maybe here in nothing-world we're the kind of group that does a cheesy team move right before we drive into the unknown. I reach out and gently punch in my agreement. Even Faye eventually joins in and bumps her fist against ours, her sharp silver raven skull ring poking into my knuckle.

"Go on, Spence," Faye says. "Drive. Get a move on before we change our minds."

) ● (

Exit 151 takes us up a gentle hill, at the top of which is a dead end surrounded by a massive abandoned quarry. Between the highway and the quarry cliff, there's a tall, utilitarian roadside structure that looks like something between an air traffic control tower and a fire lookout. There's a row of orange hazard cones surrounding it, like maybe they meant to build a wall or a barrier or something there, but they just haven't gotten around to it. Half of the cones are knocked over.

We have no idea what this place is—it's unmarked except for the number 151 on a rusty metal sign bolted onto the building near ground level. But there's a door at the base of it and it's unlocked, and that's good enough for Shel. He's practically yanking that door open as soon as we get out of the van. Inside, there's a spiral stairwell that curves all the way up to the top of the tower.

Faye immediately announces that she's staying down by the camper; she's terrified of heights and she really doesn't want to go up there. I think about staying with her, too, but in the end, I decide I have to stick with my brothers. I don't know if I'm going to be much use on whatever this expedition is, but symbolically, I want to have their backs.

I *am* a little relieved that someone is going to be staying on the outside—though I suppose the jury's out on whether Faye would actually come after us in the event that we didn't come back. There's a chance she might just get in the van and drive away, and I'm not sure if that would be such a bad idea.

"Go grab a walkie, Stacey," Spence says. "And get one for Faye, too. We'll keep them on."

I run back inside the van and grab one of our neon green plastic walkie-talkies from the shelf in Shel's office, checking that the dial is still tuned to our usual channel. Though we haven't found any sign of wi-fi or phone signal in nothing-world, our walkies still work just fine out here, and we've been keeping them with us whenever we have to split up.

We've had these things ever since we were kids, when Mom bought us two sets of two. One of the walkies was hers, and she used to use it to call us home from the playground down the road—their crappy range just about reached that far.

All of them are exactly the same; there's no way to know for sure whose handset was whose. But the one in my hands is the only one that doesn't have any scratches or scuffs on the casing, the one that obviously hasn't ever been forgotten on a playground swing or had action figures thrown on top of it in our toy box. That means this one must have been Mom's.

After she died, I used to keep my walkie by my bed, like maybe I'd hear it buzz and it would be her. I'd lie there and turn the dial back and forth, clicking around between channels, until I fell asleep listening to the crackling silence.

I blink away tears and quickly wipe my face as I clip the walkie onto my belt loop. I grab another one for Faye and throw it to her as I leave the camper.

And then my brothers and I head back to that metal door. And together, the three of us head up into the tower.

We jostle against each other in the dim light, an uncomfortable silence hanging between us as we wind our way up the narrow stairwell, our feet echoing on the corrugated metal steps. We *could* move apart; that would certainly make it easier to navigate the narrow space, but we don't. Instead, we orbit each other like magnets, hands clasped, holding on to each other's jackets, as if something terrible might happen if we move more than a foot apart. Like scared kindergartners on a rope, we hold fast to one another for courage. We really should have brought a flashlight, but none of us thought of it, and we're not turning back now.

Up we climb, the Kells siblings all in a row, oldest to youngest. Up, up, up for what feels like an hour, but is most likely about two minutes. And then, finally, we reach a worn metal landing on the upper level of the tower.

There's another door up there, with peeling blue paint and a silver push handle that looks a bit off-kilter. The door is ajar, but for a long time we just stare at it, as though we've collectively forgotten what a door does. We glance at each other breathlessly, all jangling nerves, and then Spence takes a step back as best he can and suddenly kicks the door open.

It flies open with a crash, smashing into something metallic behind it—a trash can, maybe?— and we all jump. The control room is wide open to us, and we stare some more. I don't know what I expected to see in there—probably an empty room with some consoles in it, maybe a working communication device if we're incredibly lucky. But there's something person-shaped sitting in the single operator's seat, and my heart jolts in my chest. *A dead body?* I've never seen a dead body before, and I'm not keen to break that streak now.

But no. *Wait.* They're not dead. My brain refocuses, reinterprets. The seat is slowly swinging around, its occupant staring at us curiously. They lift one of their oversize purple headphones away from their ear, peering at us as if we've just walked into their living room and interrupted their video game or something. Not like we're the *only living people within hundreds of miles of here*, barging in with a kick to the door like some damned action movie heroes because my brother always needs to be fucking dramatic.

"Hey, y'all," they say, loudly snapping a piece of gum. "Looking for someone?"

Spence's mouth drops open, and he whispers: "*God.*"

"Ah, damn. Sorry. I think God clocked off about half an hour ago." They drop the headphones, letting them hang loose around their neck as they flash us a wry grin. "So... I guess you're stuck with just me."

Spence stands with his hands clenched at his sides, like he's still not quite sure what to do. Shel's behind him, holding his little camera tripod with both hands like he might be about to take a swing. I put a hand on his shoulder, tugging him back by his jacket sleeve. But the person in the control room chair doesn't seem the least bit threatened;

in fact, they look almost amused.

"I was wonderin' when someone was finally going to show up," they say.

"Are you the one who put up that message?" Spence asks. "The emergency assistance request that we saw on the sign, at Exit 151?"

"Nnnoooo? Or...maybe yes?" They shrug. "I don't actually know what I did. I just pushed that." They point at a large red button embedded in the wall, some kind of emergency switch that used to be covered by the clear plastic casing that's now shattered on the ground just below. "That thing there said to press it in case of emergency, so I did. I figured 'everyone in the world except for me has disappeared' counts as an emergency." They squint at my brothers in the dim light. "Have you seen any other people around?"

Shel's shoulders slump a little. "No. Well... just you. You're the first one we've found."

"We saw an emergency message on the highway sign back there, so we decided to follow it," says Spence. He gestures over his shoulder in the vague direction of the highway we came from. "We've been moving west for days now, and we haven't run into anyone at all."

"Same here," the stranger says, tucking a strand of their spiky dark hair behind their ear. "My car broke down, and I've been walking—turns out that trying to hitchhike is *real* useless out here, huh? Not many cars." They grin again. "I'm glad y'all showed up, 'cause I was definitely gettin' a bit weirded out."

I look them over carefully. At first I'm convinced there's something oddly familiar about them, but I don't actually think I've ever seen them before. I'm guessing they're roughly the same age as us—probably twenty-something—with light brown skin and an androgynous face that's dominated by their strikingly arched jet-black eyebrows. Their ears are lined with almost as many piercings as Faye has, and they have a dozen tiny dangling earrings that sparkle along their lobes: shiny little cubes and holographic rainbows and rhinestones that all look incongruously colorful in the grey utility of the control tower.

They don't seem to have very much stuff with them, but there's a puffy bright purple jacket on the floor, thrown on top of a camping backpack covered in festival patches. The jacket is stenciled across the back with glittery silver text that says *THEY/THEM, HERE FOR*

MAY/HEM.

"Cool, cool, cool," Spence is saying. "Right. It's, ah... yeah, it's just so great to finally meet another person out here, huh? Just... totally awesome."

He does this ridiculous finger-guns thing at them, and I cringe a little on the inside. Spence is not the smoothest at the best of times when faced with an attractive and interesting individual. But then again, we're also dealing with the discovery that we're not alone here in nothing-world, so I can't say I really blame him for acting like a bit of a dork. This is practically a first contact situation.

"I want to take a look at this equipment and see if there's anything working," Shel says. He, on the other hand, seems to have instantly forgotten the novelty of the fact that we've found another living human, and he's straight back to business. He looks at our new friend. "Have you seen a satellite phone, or any kind of communication device in here?"

"Maybe," the stranger says. "Hypothetically, if I *had* seen a satellite phone, I would have picked it up and put it in my bag. But I would also have tried it already. Several times."

"And... hypothetically, did you receive any response?"

"What do *you* think?"

"Right." Shel nods. "And the chances of you letting us see this sat-phone for ourselves...?"

"Depends." They snap their gum. "You got a ride for me?"

Spence and Shel exchange glances.

"A ride to where?" Spence asks.

"Wherever you're going." They arch one of their perfect eyebrows. "You *are* going somewhere, right?"

"Yeah. Uh, well... I sincerely hope we are," Spence says.

Shel whispers something to Spence then, before Spence slowly nods his head. Spence looks over at me, and I'm not sure what he wants me to do. I pause, then also give an emphatic nod to affirm that the Kells family stands united in *whatever this is.*

"All right," Spence says to the stranger. "How about this, then. If you give my brother the sat-phone you found, then you're welcome to ride with us for a few days, at least. Till we figure things out. Or, uh... till we find anything else. Our camper van's just outside. Down there."

He points.

Out the curved window, I can see a long stretch of the empty highway, and our camper parked on the gravel lot below, between the half-knocked-over traffic cones that delineate the entrance to the tower. I see the red and yellow stripes painted down the sides of the camper, and the little satellite dish on the roof. I see Faye standing down there, too, leaning against the van; I can make out the shape of her blue ponytail and her black leather jacket. She's looking away from the tower, back toward the highway. We should probably buzz her on the walkie.

"Cool. Thanks a million, mate," the stranger is saying. Spence reaches out to shake their hand, and they immediately take his hand in both of theirs, squeezing it with a grateful smile. "Sounds fantastic to me."

They don't ask us anything else before they decide we're all right. We haven't even introduced ourselves. But I suppose it doesn't matter a ton who we are when we're literally the only people alive for miles. I think they would've come with us no matter what we said. And I know Spence would totally have taken them with us even if they didn't give up the sat-phone. My brother is way too soft to leave anyone behind.

They pick up their jacket from on top of their camping backpack, then fish around inside the bag until they pull out a chunky rectangular device and toss it over to Shel. "Here you go. Have at it. Doesn't work, and neither does any of the rest of the electronic junk up here. But it's all yours!"

We take a last look around the control room. Shel confirms that indeed, none of the computer consoles in the tower work, and probably haven't for years. And then, all four of us head back down to the camper van.

After dinner, I'm sitting in the van reading one of my favorite sci-fi novels. I've already read this one three times on this trip, but it's kind of relaxing to sink back into it and get invested in someone *else's* terrible problems for a while. Whatever's up with us, at least we're not on the run from an evil corporation or harboring a royal fugitive... well,

I don't *think* so, in any case. I suppose we don't know all that much about our mysterious traveling companion yet.

Next to me, Faye's lying on her cot listening to music. She's got her headphones on, but it's turned up so loud I can practically feel the bass in my chest. Shel's in his office again, doing something on his laptop. And Spence... Spence is still outside with our new friend. *Ramone*, that's what their name is. "Like the band, you know... except singular."

I peer out the open window into the encroaching dark, toward the semi-circle of our fold-out lawn chairs arranged around the campfire. Spence is stoking the fire while Ramone looks on from their cross-legged perch in one of the lawn chairs. They're wearing their purple jacket, pulled up to their neck against the evening chill.

I watch Spence snapping a pile of sticks in two over his knee before dropping them onto the fire, artfully arranging them like he knows what he's doing. I can tell he wants to impress Ramone, because he's narrating what he's doing like he's on some kind of wilderness survival show, complete with suspenseful pauses. He always narrates when he wants attention. And Ramone is indulging him, watching him intently like this campfire assembly is the most interesting thing in the world.

Then Ramone lights up a joint. They hold it out and offer it to him, and I know my brother's got it bad when he actually accepts it and takes a drag. Spence *hates* the smell of weed; just two nights ago he was grumbling at Shel for lighting up his bong inside the camper. But with Ramone, it's a different story. He's obviously into them. I wonder if he's told them he has a girlfriend back home—

I stop myself. Maybe there is no *back home* anymore. As for whether Spence technically still has a girlfriend when we're here in nothing-world... I guess that's up for debate. I'm probably not going to ask him about that.

I squint through the window, focusing on the flames as they leap across to Spence's new offering of dry wood, eating it up as eagerly as he basks in Ramone's attention. I roll my eyes, but I'm grudgingly happy for Spence. At least some of us are having fun. And as for Shel, he's been as close as he gets to giddy ever since he got his hands on that sat-phone. Never mind that a sat-phone is totally useless if there aren't any working satellites, and I don't think there are, because our

GPS hasn't worked since we got here.

Still, Shel climbed right up and mounted the sat-phone to the little dish on our camper roof when we stopped, connecting it to our local network. It's still up there, I think, its circuits humming with hope, crackling with the possibility of the unknown—like we all do.

I lie back on my cot, close my eyes, and wish for a dreamless sleep.

) ● (

I'm standing in that gas station bathroom, washing my hands, watching pink soap suds swirling off my fingers and circling down into the stainless-steel sink. There's my face in the cracked mirror, my eyes strange and haunted in the bluish glow of the flickering fluorescent bulb.

I'm wearing a faded old t-shirt, the one with the logo of the coffee shop Mom used to work at—a tacky smiling coffee bean mascot. The design is barely visible now, the plastic decal tattered and peeling. The text used to be a vibrant purple, but it's washed out to something closer to grey.

I feel faded, too. It's been so long since I felt happy, or truly hopeful about the future. I know Mom would've wanted more for us— more than this endless grief that we never seem to recover from. I'd like to think she would have been proud of us for pulling it together the way we did after she died. For having each other's backs, like we always promised we would. But the truth is that we're lost, and as much as we've tried to help each other, we're still drowning.

Spencer won't let go of how goddamn responsible he feels for everyone all the time, and he can't get out of his head long enough to decide what he wants to do with his life. Shelton has still never figured out how to talk about his feelings, so he shuts us all out and pretends he's the only one of us who's fine. And me? Mostly, I just miss Mom. I feel like I stopped moving forward the day she died, because I never got a handle on how to be a person in a world without her in it.

I think we all came on this roadtrip to try to sort things out, but so far all we've done is retreat further into our own little worlds. Tomorrow is the anniversary of Mom's death, and none of us have mentioned it, but we all know it. Five years ago, this night was the last time things were right in our world.

I turn off the tap and dry my hands on my shirt, wiping them over the smiley coffee bean on my chest. Then I open the bathroom door, tuck the plastic keyring into my pocket, and walk back out into the parking lot.

As I exit, a calico cat startles me as it jumps out of the bushes and runs toward our parked camper. It passes swiftly underneath the front tires and then weaves between the gas pumps before it disappears off again into the night. I walk in the same direction it went, toward the vending machine, where my brothers and Faye are bickering about who's going to drive.

The next day, I wake up to find Shel is already dressed and at his desk— and already in a foul mood. He's doing that thing where he swears under his breath without realizing it, mouthing a stream of curses as he types, as if he's casting some kind of magic spell over his laptop. His busted-ass laptop looks like it needs arcane arts to hold together in the first place, and part of the screen is only holding on with duct tape. His whole work area is framed by empty energy drink cans as usual, arranged in a circle like some kind of metallic henge.

As I'm grabbing my coffee mug from our dish rack, I spot the notebook that's sitting on the corner of Shel's desk. *RAMONE* is written on the cover, and a pen is sitting on top of it. Of course he sat them down to interview them yesterday the minute they got into our van, determined to get every detail out of them and piece together their path into this forsaken place the same way he's been dissecting ours. They really had no idea what they were getting into when they got on board with us. I'm sure they were *thrilled* to tell him if they remember pressing a particular sequence of buttons on a vending machine before all this shit happened.

"Morning, Shel," I say, chirping the words with the kind of exaggerated cheer that would usually get a glare out of him. But my brother doesn't even look up at me, so I palm the *RAMONE* notebook as I pass, carrying my empty mug outside.

Spence is there by the campfire again—or maybe *still*—stirring up porridge over the fire in our single good pan. He's sprinkling sugar into it and swirling the wooden spoon round and round far too dramatically for the mundane task at hand. It looks like he's already made coffee for everyone too; there's a steaming thermos sitting at the edge of the fire pit. Guess he's trying to impress Ramone again. Or still.

We put up our all-weather tent for Ramone when we parked up yesterday, since there isn't really room for another person to sleep in the van. There isn't even really room for the four of us, if Spence wasn't sleeping on the front seat. I wonder where Ramone slept before they met us, since they said they abandoned their car. I wonder a lot of things about them, actually. But I'll leave it to Shel to grill them. Maybe it's already written in the book.

I see that the tent has already been disassembled and rolled up next to the camper, and Ramone is sitting on one of the lawn chairs next to Faye. The two of them are both watching Spence make his dramatic porridge with blank looks on their faces. Ramone has Spence's sunglasses on, and their hair looks *way* messier than yesterday, like they haven't bothered to run a comb through it yet. To come to think of it, Spence looks pretty dishevelled too, and he's wearing the exact same shirt as last night. I wonder if he spent the night outside—or maybe with Ramone, in the tent.

I don't go over to the fire pit. Instead, I sit down on the little metal step that hangs from the side door of the camper, and I open up Shelton's notebook on my lap. The first page is filled with a long scrawl of underlined questions in Shel's terrible handwriting, and his notes about Ramone's answers below.

He recorded the whole interview on his computer, too—he even set up his special podcasting mic for the occasion—but he's obsessed with keeping analog records of all the things we do now.

Last known contact with outside world?

    Received text from friend at 10:40pm (didn't answer bc was driving)

    When did mobile phone die?

    →*Tried to call roadside assistance on Jun 14th around 11pm, but NO SIGNAL*

    → *Phone must have died btwn 10:40 & 11pm*

    → *Also noticed GPS was not working just after 11 (same as us!!)*

    Last known direction of travel?

→WEST!!! (Of fucking course it was)
Where did car break down? Near Legend Roadstop?
→Remembers driving past a gas station just before car died - maybe this was Legend Roadstop??? Can't remember more details.
→Tried to walk back to the gas station when car died, should have been a couple mins to get back, but the gas station was no longer there!!!! IMPORTANT!!
Did the map change?
→Didn't notice the map had changed (Walking!) However, SEE ABOVE, GAS STATION WAS NO LONGER THERE!!! - this suggests map change happened

My skin prickles as I read. I know all this same weird stuff already happened to us, and I've seen some fucked up shit with my own eyes. Like a drone disappearing out of thin air. But somehow, seeing it all written out like this—hearing that it happened to another person—just seems a million times creepier.

"Hey, Stace!" Spence calls out when he finally notices me out there. "Come over here! We're talking plans for today."

I quickly shove the notebook under my hoodie before I walk over to the fire pit.

"We're gonna keep driving west, I think," Spence says when I sit down on the grass. "We've all agreed that seems like the most logical thing to do. I think we need to keep following this highway, so at least we sort-of know where we are. We'll keep pulling over if we see something on a nearby exit, or to grab supplies and fuel up, but otherwise we'll stick to the highway and just keep going... until we come to a major city or something. If there are other survivors, that's probably where they'll be."

"Sure," I say with a shrug. He's repeating this part for Ramone's benefit, I'm sure, because this has been our plan all along. To keep going until we get to a city—if we ever do. But when Spence says "a major city" like he's not exactly sure *which* city it's gonna be... that's true. We really have no idea where we are.

According to the old map, if we stayed on the same highway we should've passed *several* cities by now. But they weren't there. We haven't even passed any signs for towns at all. We've pulled off at lots of exits, but it's all just roadstops and gas stations, the kind of thing you find when you're in that void between cities, where you drive and drive for hours and it all looks the same.

I feel like it's a bit weird to call ourselves "survivors," when no apocalypse really happened. We don't even know that anyone *died*. For all we know, we're the only people anything happened to. There's no zombies, no asteroid strike, no nuclear bomb, no deadly virus, so what did we survive, exactly? We're not survivors so much as... *existers*.

Every day we drive west, and there's just more and more highway that looks basically the same. But nobody dares to suggest that we're never going to find a city. We should've been on the coast by now, and we all know it. I guess we'll see for sure in a couple more days.

"Sounds good," says Ramone. "Driving west. Yeah. That sounds fine to me."

That afternoon, we pull over to check out a little roadside motel. Shel wants to check for internet access and look around again for some kind of communication method.

As soon as we turn off of the highway, we can already see the pink brick building just over the ridge. The sign out front is a huge, bright yellow sun with SUNNYVIEW MOTEL written under it in a swirly pink font, and below that there's one of those old-school board signs that you can stick plastic letters into:

WI-FI
POOL
AIRCON
ARCADE

The whole place looks familiar in the way that all roadside motels look familiar. This is exactly the sort of place you pull up to when you just want a bed with room to roll over in it, and a chance to take a lukewarm motel shower.

We park up and pile out of the van, and Spence hands out the walkie-talkies—since we only have four of them, he announces that Ramone's just going to have to stay with somebody at all times. Of course, he's subtly volunteering himself, and they don't object. It's sweet how Spence keeps looking behind him to smile at Ramone, almost like he's making sure they're still there.

Spence might be romantically awkward, but he's the kind of guy who's pretty much always dating *somebody*. He rarely stays single for long. And yet, he never seems to get all that invested. I've hardly even met his current girlfriend, Annie, the concert musician he started seeing a few months ago. And he's been so busy working on our camper since the warm weather came that I doubt he spent much time with her before we left. I wonder if Annie's been trying to call my brother this whole time, not knowing that we quite literally fell off the map.

The five of us cross the parking lot toward the motel's pink gate, walking single file again like we're going on some kind of field trip. Faye is totally that kid who didn't want to go; she's at the back looking annoyed, kicking at the little pieces of concrete that have fallen out of the crumbling front path. I know she's not convinced that we should have picked up Ramone, but we were never going to leave them behind, so she's grudgingly accepted that we've got a new crew member now.

Mostly, I think Faye just wants Shelton to stop talking about disappearing gas stations and whether Ramone saw the same full moon we did and whether it might be possible to pinpoint the exact second when the phone signal dropped. While Shel was interviewing Ramone, Faye sat on her cot with her headphones on and her music cranked up, pretending that none of it was happening. I wish I was as good at pretending.

Inside the Sunnyview Motel, we go into the little lobby and head to the reception desk first, because of course we do. I feel like some deeply ingrained part of us is still hard-wired to obey the rules of society, the same way we still put the turn signal on when we're about to take an exit. We have no choice but to ring that bell and wait at the desk, *just in case*, as if we're just here checking in like five Very Normal Guests.

We stand there shuffling our feet, staring at the empty reception area for what feels like an appropriate amount of time to say "we made an effort" before we just walk on back there. Unsurprisingly, nobody comes to check us in.

Finally, Shel goes behind the desk and starts scooping up all of the room keys from the wall. There aren't that many keys, since this place is small and only has a dozen rooms. There were no empty hooks; all twelve keys seem to be accounted for. Each keyring is stamped with the same canary yellow sun logo from the sign out front, with a bright pink room number on the back.

I do a quick recon on the rest of the desk—everything is utterly unsurprising. There's a pink plastic landline phone sitting on the counter, but there's no dial tone. The paper reservation logbook sitting on the desk is completely empty; there are no dates or notes or guest names written on any of its pages. It's just a completely blank book. I pull out my Sharpie and write my name neatly on the first page: *Stacey M. Kells.* Definitely a compulsion at this point.

"Okay, the three of us are gonna go upstairs to check through the rooms," Shel says, indicating himself and Spence and Ramone. He dumps the pile of keyrings on the desk, a heap of yellow plastic suns. "We can split these up between us and we'll check inside 'em all. As always, look for anything with a date on it, any personal items, especially phones or computers. And keep an eye out for anything weird." Then he turns to me and Faye. "You two, you'll go check out the main floor, same deal. Then we can meet back out front when we're done."

"Well, fuck, I guess *we've* been told," Faye says sarcastically. "Don't remember electing *you* the roadtrip dictator."

"Well, technically dictators don't actually *have* to be elected, do they?" Ramone says. They snap their gum. "Isn't that kind of the definition of a dictator?"

Spence and Shel both laugh, and I wince inwardly. Ramone may have won Spence's heart already, and Shel's cool with them for now because they shared the sat-phone—but they *really* don't want to get on Faye's bad side if they're sticking with us. And I don't think they're off to a great start.

"Oh, yeah. You're right. I think I meant a *dick*," Faye says with a withering glare at Shel. She digs her nails into my arm, turns around and drags me after her down the main hallway. "Let's go, Stace. Let's get this shit over with."

I look back at Spence and Shel and Ramone divvying up the pile of keys before they head out the front door toward the rooms. They're all still laughing. The motel rooms are arranged along the upper floor, accessed by two staircases on the outside of the building, and I kind of wish we'd all just stuck together. I wish I was going back outside with them, instead of deeper into this building, because there's a *real* creepy vibe in here. And Faye is *pissed.*

The place only gets weirder the further in we go. We do a super quick walk around the main floor, taking a cursory look at everything, even though we both think it's fundamentally pointless. It's mostly empty space, just a bunch of hallways with no doors, and one long conference room that's full of stacked-up folding chairs.

We don't ever leave the main hallway; we just peek into the others, and I keep looking back to make sure I can still see the edge of the reception desk as we go. This whole place looks like a photo shoot from one of those tumblr blogs about liminal spaces. The kind of architecture that looks totally regular if you squint one way, and almost non-Euclidean from another angle.

"Does this building seem bigger to you than, you know... how big it should be?" Faye asks. She's still holding on to my arm pretty tightly, and Faye is *not* a touchy person.

"Yeah, totally. There's just so many *hallways* everywhere. So there's twelve rooms upstairs, but like thirty empty hallways down here? Where the fuck do all of these even go?"

"I don't know, and I'm not finding out." Faye says. "We had a quick look, that's good enough for me. We didn't see anything, nothing here, let's go. I'm done. This is weird as hell."

I'm still kind of intrigued to look around, in a morbidly fascinated way. But not quite enough to venture into one of those hallways without Faye, walkie-talkie or not. If Shel wants a more detailed report, I guess he'll just have to brave the labyrinth in here himself.

We backtrack to the reception area, and I follow Faye outside into the front courtyard of the motel. I'm surprised how relieved I feel when the warm desert air hits my face. I hadn't realized how *cold* it was in there. The sign did promise there was AC, and that's obviously still running, like all of the other electrics we've come across. The only stuff that's *not* working is anything that would let us communicate with the outside world.

As soon as we get outdoors, I can hear Spence laughing uproariously at something on the upper floor, and I think I can hear

Ramone and Shel's voices too, unintelligible. The three of them are halfway through opening the row of rooms, because six of the doors up there are open. I guess they haven't found anything creepy, or else it's creepy *and* funny. Either way, I'm just glad to hear my brother laughing like that again. He hasn't laughed nearly as often in the past few years as he used to before Mom died... though I suppose none of us have.

"You wanna go take a look 'round the back?" Faye suggests, pointing toward the side of the motel. "Maybe there's a vending machine back there that Shel can ask us about fifteen thousand times."

"Oh, don't *even*. If there is, I don't fucking want to know."

We start walking around toward the back anyway, because there's nothing much else for us to do. We pass by the outdoor pool, gated off by another pink fence, with a row of pink loungers spread out around it. It looks incredibly normal, all clear and blue and perfect, like on the front of a postcard. But as I stare at the little ripples on the surface of the pool water, for some reason I suddenly get a flash of that cursed party at Marky-O's, and his backyard pool. I don't know what the fuck made me think of *that*.

Faye is still kicking pieces of concrete out of the paved path as we go, stopping to work a few out with the toe of her boot and then launching a volley of little rocks toward the wall of the motel. I stomp on a loose corner and kick some pieces out too. It feels oddly good, and I take some small satisfaction in seeing them scatter against the wall, just like I expect them to. At least gravity is still normal. And we can still break things.

I wonder if wanting to break things is some kind of primordial, universal 'am I real' test.

And then, Faye pauses in her tracks, her pointy black nails digging hard into my arm. "Shhh, shhh! Stop, Stace, listen!" She tilts her head. "D'you hear that?"

We both come to a full stop. I blink slowly, and for a second I only hear the soft, perpetual rustle of the desert wind. Then I look at the motel again. There's a single narrow window on this part of the building, standing half-open in the pink brick wall, and I can hear—

"God*damn* it. I *hate* this fucking song!" Faye growls.

I think I'm going to throw up. *No way, no way, no way, that can't possibly be—*

But it is. Coming from the window... that's the chorus of "Cat Said Meow."

) ● (

I burst away from Faye and I run to the window, sticking my head inside. As my eyes adjust to the dim light, I see what's in there: a games arcade, a retro one, the kind I've only seen in movies. The kind with the car-racing machines that you can sit in, and the Dance Dance Revolution booths with the arrow pads on the floor, and all the old joystick games like Pac-Man and shit. On the floor, there's one of those nineties geometric carpets that you get in movie theaters, with all the colorful shapes on it. There's an uncarpeted strip of bare cement that runs between the game areas, lit by a strip of neon LEDs.

"Hello?" I call through the window. "Is someone in here?"

But there's nobody inside. There's just this weird feeling of *emptiness*, like a sense of abandonment, despite the fact that I can still hear the music playing. This arcade isn't just closed for the day; no, it feels like there hasn't been anyone here for a very long time.

The song carries on over tinny speakers, the repeated refrain transporting me back to that horrible night at Marky-O's party, and tears prick at my eyes. How the fuck is this *possible*? I need to see where it's coming from. Before I can think, I hoist myself up onto the sill and haul myself inside.

Behind me, I can hear Faye shouting at me to stop, asking what the hell I'm doing, but I don't care. I wriggle through the window and fall inelegantly through to the other side, landing on my knees on the worn-down carpet. As I land, I see a flicker of movement from the corner of my eye, a long shadow crossing the wall to my left, and I freeze. Is somebody over there?

But a moment later, I see exactly what it was. There's a cat in here—a goddamn *cat!*—and now it's darting away out of sight, slipping under one of the pinball machines. I think it was a calico, like the cat I saw at the Legend Roadstop, but that's probably just my brain playing tricks on me. I'm doing that looking-for-patterns thing again. It's not as if I got a great look at either of them. They're two similarly-colored cats that I saw for all of like two seconds each. *Not everything means something, Stacey.*

But this *is* the first animal we've come across in nothing-world, and that's got to count for something. I stay crouched down, looking behind the nearby machines to see where the cat went.

"Stacey, get out of there!" Faye hisses from the window. "What the hell, dude!"

"Hang on." I raise my hand. "I thought I saw…"

Faye sticks her head in. "Hey! Is that a fucking *cat?*"

I follow her gaze, and I see where it's gone. It's sitting next to a yellow coin-operated jukebox with glowing letters on it that say MEGA-MEGA-HITS. The track that's currently playing is lit up on a warped, crappy little screen like they have on karaoke machines.

Cat Said Meow.

Somehow, that jukebox must've been stuck on one song for god knows how long. Has *this* song really been playing on loop since the world turned sideways? Maybe the nothing-world is some kind of twisted afterlife. Maybe I'm in my own personal hell.

The calico cat runs away into the shadows again as I get up and jog over to the machine. I lean down and stick my hand behind it, and I yank the thick black electrical plug out of the wall. The music cuts out abruptly, and the lights on the machine sputter out. *Fuck that.*

I dust my hands off and look further into the room, where the rows of game machines seem to go on further than I can see. How is all of this even *in* here? This room alone looks as big as a warehouse, bigger than the whole motel.

"Don't. Get the fuck out of there, Stace," Faye says from the window. "Come back. Don't go where I can't see you."

I take one last look into the distance, and I swear I see two shiny cat eyes blink at me from the shadows. Then I turn back around, and I let Faye help me crawl back out the window.

We briefly debate staying at the motel overnight, but ultimately we all agree that we'd feel better going back to the camper. I'm relieved when we vote unanimously to leave, and to drive on as far as we can while we have the light.

In the van, I tell Shel about the endless arcade we saw, just in case that's somehow going to be relevant to his *research*. He makes note of the fact that we saw a cat, scribbling it down next to the rest of our observations about the creepy motel. I don't mention the jukebox, and Faye flat out refuses to talk about any of it.

There's still talk of us 'probably making it to the city' soon, which at this point is basically a collective delusion we've decided to embrace. It's like Spence says, how long can we keep driving west before we get *somewhere*? I don't think any of us actually want to know the answer to that. But so long as we keep moving, we can pretend it makes a difference.

Shelton's *research* now covers every inch of the wall in the middle compartment of the camper, some of it several layers deep. He has continued to "keep track of things"—that is to say, he's constantly documenting all the strange shit happening around us that's scrambling our rational brains. Sometimes, I see Faye half-closing her eyes while she gets something out of the kitchenette, as if she literally can't bear to look over at Shel's office.

I peruse the chaos of his sprawling wall display while I boil water and wait for my instant ramen to soften. I stir the noodles back and forth in their laminated cup, letting my gaze skim idly over the latest facts and figures. There's this one chart where Shel's been comparing the reading on the odometer each day to how fast the gas is depleting from the tank, estimating our van's mileage. But none of us really need to see the math to know it doesn't add up; there's been times where we've driven for days on the same tank, and other times I hear Spence swearing under his breath at the blinking gas light when it feels like we've just recently stopped.

Inconsistent, Shel has written in the margin. And lower down the page, *No discernible pattern*. On yesterday's entry, there's just a scrawled *WHY THE FUCK??* with a bunch of underlines beneath it. He pressed the pen down so hard that it almost tore through the page. I guess this is the closest Shel will come to keeping a personal diary, this barometer of his mood laid bare on a wrinkled sheet of lined paper taped to a camper wall.

Next to the mileage chart, he's pinned up one of Faye's doodles—or maybe she put it up there herself. Two hands clenched into fists, middle fingers up, with the letters ROAD TRIP tattooed above bleeding knuckles. The raised fingernails are painted black, with pointed tips just like Faye's own. The black ovals are slightly detached, I notice, floating above the empty nail beds like two disembodied heads. This is what we are now, all of us: a collage of images and numbers that sit askew from reality. Recognizable, but not quite making sense.

Just as I finish eating my ramen and chuck the packaging into our small trash bag, the camper van starts slowing down. We're exiting from the highway. The sun is already gone, and we don't usually stop in the evenings until we're going to park up for the night. But we're totally out of soft drinks in the mini-fridge, and we need more flashlight batteries, so Spence has been on the lookout for a convenience store.

"Who's comin' with me, hmm?" he calls out when we pull over. I can see he's already turning around to look at Ramone in the passenger seat, but I dart through the bead curtain, grabbing his sleeve to cut in first.

"Me! I'll go with you," I say quickly. "I want to stretch my legs."

Honestly, I just want to talk to Spence alone for a minute, because he's been glued to Ramone's hip ever since we picked them up.

"All right, cool." Spence says. "C'mon, Stace. We'll make it a quick dash, okay?"

He leaves the keys hanging in the ignition and hops out. I don't bother with going to the back to collect the milk crates, since we're just grabbing a couple of things. I just slam the side door open and follow after him.

"Check if they have some Dr Pepper!" Faye shouts from the van as we head for the store. "Spence! Did you hear me?"

"Yeah, yeah, I got it, Faye!" Spence yells back over his shoulder. "Dr Pepper, just like the last thirteen years!" But there's no annoyance on his face; in fact, he's grinning. Spence has been in such a good mood since we picked up Ramone that I can't even be mad about him not talking to me very much.

I can already see there's nobody inside the store through the brightly lit front window. Other than the fact that it's empty like everything else in nothing-world, it's a roadstop much like all the rest of them. There's a couple of picnic tables on the little patch of lawn out front, and a basic convenience store setup inside. The kind of place that could be literally anywhere.

"So, let's hear an official statement—you're real into Ramone, huh?" I elbow Spence in the ribs like I used to do when we were kids, making silly kiss noises at him.

He grins wider as soon as I say their name, and I can't believe it, but my brother is actually *blushing*. As we step into the rectangle of light that's spilling out of the store window, I see his face go beet red, and he laughs sheepishly. "Yeah, I guess I am, a little bit. Is it that obvious?"

"Tch, only to every living person in a fifteen-mile radius. Which, you know... to be fair, I guess is not *that* many people."

He laughs. "Yeah. Well... I do really think Ramone and I might have something going on," he says. "Guess it only took an actual *I'm-the-last-man-on-earth* situation for me to pull someone that cool, huh? Not like it could happen in the real world."

I open the front door and we step into the store. It's got the usual useless jingling chime over the door, echoing into the empty space. Everything sounds strange here in nothing-world, like it's too much and too little all at the same time.

"What about Annie?" I ask him. I haven't broached the subject of his real-world girlfriend since we've been here, and I kind of regret mentioning Annie as soon as I say her name. To come to think of it, Spence hasn't talked about her in a while, even before the roadtrip.

"Yeahhh...nah, Annie was *not* that cool," he says. "And besides, she broke up with me. She dumped me by text, actually. Classic."

"Oh. Oh, wow... I'm sorry, dude. I didn't know about that. When?"

"A couple weeks before we left."

"Damn." I scan my brother's face for any trace of anger or disappointment, but there's none there. "Why didn't you say anything to me? Did you tell Shel?"

"Nah." He shrugs. "It didn't seem that important, honestly. It's not like she ever hung out with us or anything. We broke up, oh well, it happens. I didn't let myself get too down about it. Me an' Annie were never gonna work out, anyway. We're just... *different people*."

"Aren't we all?" I ask. "Different people?"

"Yeah. Yeah, I guess. That *is* kind of a funny expression, when you really think about it."

We split up at the end of the main aisle, and I head over to grab the soda while Spence goes to look for batteries. The drinks are in the last aisle at the very back, and I scan the shelves quickly. Most of the stuff is in good supply, and there's not a single gap on most of the shelves back here, as if the products have recently been restocked. But the shelf where the Dr Pepper should be is completely empty; there's just a space with a price label and not a single remaining bottle. I grab a couple of big bottles of Coke instead, and some cans of root beer, picking up as many as I can carry.

"Hey," Spence says, coming around the corner to me. "Found 'em. You get the soda?" He's holding a variety pack of batteries, the kind that has some of all the different sizes.

"Yeah. But there's no Dr Pepper, it's all sold out. You gonna be the one to tell Faye?"

"Oh, no way!" He shakes his head and makes an expression of mock horror. "This is the end, isn't it? *This* is what's gonna send Faye over the edge and finally make her murder us all."

I laugh, and we start walking together toward the exit. Our little two-person mission is ending already, and I feel like I need to say one more sincere thing to my brother before we're back in the van, back to pretending we're still looking for a city that's never there.

"For the record, I *do* think Ramone would still be into you in the real world," I say. "You're not so bad."

"Ha. Well, thanks for the vote of confidence, kiddo." He puts an arm around me and squeezes, and I realize I'm actually smiling a genuine smile. I headbutt his shoulder with the top of my head in place of hugging him back, since my arms are full of soda. I probably should have brought one of those milk crates after all.

We're about to head out with our stuff when Spence pauses to grab a bag of Doritos from the rack near the front as he passes by. "Damn. This still feels so weird, just *taking* shit, doesn't it?" he says. "I always kinda feel like we should leave some money on the counter or something. Or like, a note that says *Sorry, IOU for some Doritos.*"

I nod. "Oh, for sure. Yeah. This one time, I even rang myself up! I put a five-dollar bill into the till, and I—" I look back toward the cash register as I'm saying it. And I stop in my tracks, nearly dropping all of the soft drinks.

There's a jumbo caramel chocolate bar sitting right next to the register.

"Stace? What's wrong?"

"Oh my *god...* Spence, hang on a second, I have to—"

With shaking hands, I dump the drinks onto the counter and run around to the register side. One of the bottles of Coke rolls away and falls onto the floor, but I don't care, I don't care, I have to *see.*

I grab the chocolate bar and I scan it with the wand: $2.78.

I type in a five-dollar tender.

Change due: $2.22.

The register bangs open. And there's a single five-dollar bill in it.

When we get back to the van, Spence doesn't say anything to the group. He doesn't even say hi to Ramone. He completely ignores Faye asking if we got the Dr Pepper, he ignores Shel asking if we got the batteries, and he doesn't say a word to me either. He just gets behind the wheel, slams on the gas, and peels out of the parking lot, back onto the highway, going in the same direction we've always been going. And we drive west.

The others whisper to each other, and look at me quizzically, but I just shrug like I have no idea what's up with him. We've all had our little breakdowns, so they probably figure he just needs some space for one reason or another. I desperately want to say something to them, but the words don't come, and I feel like I should probably wait to tell them anything until I can talk to Spence again.

Spence still thinks I'm wrong—that somehow I didn't see what I think I saw in that store. He says it's possible that there's more than one convenience store with a single bill in the register, and that same chocolate bar left behind on the counter, and I suppose that's technically true.

But Spence doesn't know everything. Because on the way back to the camper van, we walked past the graffitied picnic table, and I *looked.* The edge of the table was just caught by the circular glow of the streetlight at the side of the parking lot.

Stacey M. Kells

Shelton A. Kells

Spencer J. Kells

Faye Weatherby is still a jerk. That's how I know this is real.

Spence keeps driving all night, and when daylight is close to breaking, we still haven't stopped. He won't slow down or give anyone else the wheel. He just stares at the highway ahead of him and drives west.

In his office, Shel has been up all night too, doing something on his laptop and talking to Faye, who's sitting on the floor next to his desk. Faye's drawing an elaborate tattoo design in her sketchbook, her pencil *skritch-skritch-skritching* over the rough paper so loudly that I can hear it even in the back. When I close my eyes, it sounds like something is in the camper walls trying to scratch its way in, and I shudder.

At some point, Ramone comes to sit in the back compartment with me, and I think it's the first time I've ever talked to them alone. Somehow, I feel the deep-seated need to defend Spence's image to Ramone. He wouldn't have wanted them to witness this, him not having it together.

"Spence really is a great guy," I tell them. I take off my glasses and set down the novel I was reading. "He's not usually like this. He's just... kind of stressed out right now. The shit that's happening is all so weird, so I think we all just—"

"Hey, hey. It's cool." Ramone holds up a hand. "I'm not judging or anything. I really like your brother." The corner of their lip is quirking up, and their smile is easy—*fond,* even. "Don't worry. I know Spence is a good dude."

I smile back at them, the vise around my chest unclenching a little.

"I don't say it to Spence enough, but I *am* grateful," I tell them. "He's so good to us. When our mom died... he gave up his university acceptance to take care of me. And he's been doing it ever since. He really deserves someone to look out for him for once."

Ramone reaches over and squeezes my hand. "I got you," they say. "I promise. And I appreciate it, too—him taking me in, all of you letting me travel with you like this? You had no reason to trust me."

As they clasp my hand, I look down, and the first thing I see is their slightly chipped neon manicure: bright glittery polish with silver moon phases stenciled in the center of each nail. The nail art has held up surprisingly well. But then my eyes skirt up to their inner arm, where a few inches of their light brown skin are exposed below their rolled-up sleeve. A faint ladder of criss-crossed scars runs up their arm, starting just above their wrist and disappearing beneath the edge of the fabric.

I know they see me looking, but they don't pull their hand away from mine, and they don't move to tug their sleeve down. They don't react the way I usually do when I see someone *look*. They just squeeze my hand tighter, as I wordlessly pull up the sleeve of my hoodie with my other hand, exposing the similar marks on my own arm.

"When my mom died... I think...somehow I just needed to prove to myself that I was still real," I whisper, blinking back tears. "I thought about asking Faye to tattoo over it for me this summer but... I haven't felt ready yet."

I don't know why I'm telling them this when I've never even talked to my brothers about it. I guess I've just never been able to put it into words.

"Hey, things take the time they take," Ramone says. "Maybe one day you'll cover up the past with something new and beautiful, and it'll feel right. But you don't *have* to." They look at me with a warm smile. "You know... my abuelo told me once that scars are there because you healed. And when you think about it like that... that's kind of beautiful all on its own."

I sniffle into my sleeve, and they hug me, and I wish I could say I feel better afterwards. But mostly, I just feel *seen*.

Maybe this is what feeling real is like.

I dry my hands on the tacky coffee-bean shirt and walk out of the gas station bathroom, tucking the plastic keyring into my pocket. The calico cat startles me as it hops out of the bushes, scampering off toward our parked camper. It runs underneath, then emerges out the other side and weaves its way around the gas pumps, appearing and disappearing from my view like a little specter.

And there are my brothers and Faye, standing in the glow of the vending machine, trying to buy a soda while arguing about who's going to drive.

Spencer is picking through the cupholder change that Faye's got in her hand, and he's feeding money into the machine as I approach. Faye hits the button for a Dr Pepper, but no soda drops out. All the change tumbles back down into the return slot, and she squats down to collect it.

She counts it out. "Ah, dammit. I think it ate one of our quarters!"

"It's broken," Spencer says with a sigh. "Look here. Says *ERROR*." He turns to Faye. "Forget it. Just go back in and buy a Dr Pepper inside."

"No, wait. Hang on, there's an art to this. Let me show you," says Shel. "There's always a trick to these things...you just need to drop the coins in slowly, and... hold..." He presses down the Dr Pepper button with one hand and holds it down as he starts feeding the rest of the change in again with the other hand. Faye passes the coins to him one by one.

"Listen, Spence, all I was saying before is that you could let the rest of us drive more than once in a while," Faye says, swiftly picking up the thread of their ongoing argument as soon as there's a silence. "You really think nobody else can handle your precious camper? What do you think is going to happen if someone else drives? You've got to stop being such a control freak and relax. I thought this trip was supposed to be, like, a bonding exercise."

"A *bonding exercise?*" Shel rolls his eyes. "Sure, Faye. We doing trust falls or something?" He looks down, realizing his attempt at cajoling the vending machine has failed. This time, no change returns at all, and no soda falls out either. He hammers the button repeatedly, to no avail. "Oh, goddammit, *come on!*"

"Shut up, Shel," Faye says. "Thanks for your sarcasm. I wasn't even talking to you! You know, you are so fucking emotionally constipated, you don't even know what you're— oh, please, *here*, just move out of the way." She elbows him aside, then takes a little step back to shift her weight, lining up her foot to kick the metal panel at the bottom of the machine.

I catch one last glimpse of the calico cat, disappearing into the shadows beyond the gas pumps.

When the sun is up, I walk unsteadily through the still-moving camper, making my way through Shel's office. Ramone's asleep on Faye's cot, Shel's asleep in his sleeping bag under the desk... but Faye is gone from her spot on the floor.

I push my way through the second set of bead curtains to the front, and to my surprise, Faye is driving now—Spence must finally have pulled over at some point and switched with her. He's in the passenger seat now, fast asleep, his head tilted to the side against the window, snoring quietly. The bag of Doritos sits open on his knee, and his hand is in it, like he literally passed out mid-snack. Just as well he finally let someone else take over driving.

I remember how I used to throw a little Nerf ball at Spence's head to wake him up when we were kids, and how mad he would get. And how Mom would just shake her head at us disapprovingly, with that half-smile that said she secretly thought it was hilarious. I look down at Spence sleeping, breathing softly with his mouth open, and I see his child-self in his face... and suddenly, my brother's twelve years old again, and Mom's totally about to tell him off for eating Doritos for breakfast—

And then, Faye *slams* on the brakes.

I trip and fall forward, catching myself on Spence's shoulder as I pitch headfirst over the seat and nearly smash my nose on the dash.

I scream as I fall, and Spence screams too, sitting up with a start. Behind me, I hear all our plastic dishes clatter loudly to one side in the kitchenette cubby, and Shelton gasps from his office.

Spencer has a death-grip on my wrist where he's caught me. "Dammit, Stacey! I keep telling you not to walk around when we're moving!" he shouts. "Do you want to fly through the damn windshield?"

I'm sprawled halfway into the front seat between him and Faye, with my feet sticking up behind me like a cartoon character. The

Doritos have exploded all over the place; there are chips scattered on the dashboard and on Spence's lap and all across the floor.

"What...the...*fuck*," Faye whispers. But she's not looking at me or Spence at all. Instead, she's staring out the window with something between awe and horror, her mouth open, pressing both of her palms to the glass.

In front of us, arching over the highway, is an LED sign with a scrolling orange message on it.

EMERGENCY ASSISTANCE REQUESTED AHEAD – EXIT 151

We go up the stairs to the control tower single file, as tense as we were the last time. Faye comes with us this time around, at Spence's insistence that we have to stay together. She's the only one who hasn't been up here before. She walks up with her eyes closed, her hand gripping Shel's sleeve with white knuckles.

We all stop on the little landing, clustering close together and staring at the closed blue door.

"Is this the part where you drop-kick it open for some reason?" I whisper to Spence, my voice shaking as I force a smile. Maybe Faye's not the only one with a weird nervous laugh.

"Go on, then," Ramone says, squeezing his arm. "Do it."

Spence steps forward and tests the handle. It turns easily, and he opens the door all of a quarter-inch. He leans over slowly, anxiously, like he's willing himself to peek through the crack... but then he changes his mind at the last moment. He jerks his head back, and instead he kicks the door open, just like he did when we were here before.

The door smashes into the trash can behind it with that same metallic *clang*, revealing the exact same room that we saw when we found Ramone. The chair where Ramone sat in front of the lifeless consoles is empty. Under the red button on the wall, the detritus of its smashed plastic casing is still strewn across the floor below.

As we enter the control room, Faye clutches Shel's arm, angling herself away from the wide crescent of the window so she doesn't have to see the long drop, her face buried against his jacket. Her fingers are digging into his denim sleeve like claws.

"It's the same," I whisper. "Identical. Look, the emergency button thing is busted open."

"Maybe this is a different control tower," Spence says. "I mean, there's probably like, a standard design for these or something, right? It's not the kind of thing that they'd do much redesigning on."

"But the exit number—" I start.

"It's a different section of the highway, Stacey! Maybe the numbers repeat," Spence persists, his voice rising. "We don't know for sure."

I look out the window to where our camper van is parked far below. We're between the abandoned quarry cliff and the highway, just like before. There are the exact same orange traffic cones surrounding the entry to the tower as the last time, the same half of them still knocked over, the same half of them still standing up. Same, same, same.

"Spence is right," Shel says. "We don't know anything for sure yet. This is all hypothetical."

My pulse is rushing in my ears, and I feel faint. Shel doesn't know what we saw inside the convenience store. He doesn't know what I saw on the picnic table.

Ramone is kneeling down beside the trash can. "Oh, *shit*," they whisper, their voice awed. "No, this is definitely the same tower we were in before. Look at this!" They reach into the garbage and pull out the only thing that's in there: an empty package of strawberry gummy bears. "I ate these while I was up here the first time. This is mine."

"Oh my god, oh my god, oh my god," Faye is repeating.

I know for a fact that Faye doesn't believe in a god. None of us do—well, I suppose I'm not sure about Ramone. But they're just words, anyway. Words we all say that don't mean anything. Has anything *ever* meant anything?

Not everything means something, Stacey.

Maybe we're all losing our minds out here in nothing-world. I feel like my head's on wrong, with all this *nothing* slowly pulling us to pieces. I feel like my atoms are scattering like those Doritos, like my neurons are no longer firing quite right. There are stars at the edges of my vision.

"I need to get some air," Faye says. She snatches the gummy bear wrapper out of Ramone's hand and hurls it back into the trash can, then she bolts out the door. We hear her Docs clanging all the way down the spiral staircase, and then the slam of the metal door at the bottom of the tower as she heads outside. I look out the window to see her emerge, and I watch her storming over to the camper.

"Let's go. Back to the van, everybody, right now," Spence orders, in his most authoritative Mom-voice that brokers no discussion. "We're going." We stare at each other in silence for a moment, and then we wordlessly head back down the stairs.

For once, when we get back in the van, nobody talks about how far it might still be to the city.

But still, we drive. We drive west.

As night is falling, we give up and pull over to make camp. Spence builds a fire and we sit around on our folding lawn chairs, sipping warm beer and mostly talking about other things. Now that we can't talk about 'getting to the city' anymore, we've apparently fallen back to pretending we're on a normal camping trip, conspicuously avoiding The Topic.

Spence flips hot dogs on our camp grill, spinning them artfully with a fork, in that exaggerated way that he does pretty much everything when Ramone is watching him. He's narrating in a dramatic voice now, like he's on a cooking show, even though one of those hot dogs totally just fell in the dirt and all we've got is half a loaf of bread to use instead of hot dog buns. Bread that's somehow still fresh—as fresh as convenience-store white bread ever tastes. Bread with no expiry date printed on the package.

I wonder if our imaginary reality show audience thinks Spence's goofy antics to impress Ramone are funny, or kind of pathetic. Maybe there's a hashtag about it. Or a drinking game. But I meant what I said to my brother when we were in that store aisle, and what I said to Ramone when we talked: whatever his faults, Spence is really not so bad. I hope he's got a little fan club somewhere out there.

None of us broach The Topic until after we've finished eating and another round of beers has been brought around. It's Faye who finally breaks and says it. "Soooo… we've obviously just been going around in a big loop, right? We're driving in circles. Which means… we haven't actually been going west at all, have we?"

"We *have* been going west this whole time, to the best we can tell. Confirmed by compass, but also by the position of the sun," Spence says, as if repeating it will make it true. "We should've been on the coast ages ago."

Faye takes a long drink of her beer. "Right. But we're obviously right back where we started, Spence. *Should've* doesn't mean a damn thing here."

"We just need more data," Shel declares. "We need to keep collecting records about what we're doing. Think harder. Try to find *patterns,* solve the puzzle." He takes a deep breath. "I'm pretty sure we've been *jumping around in time* sometimes, I've said that since the beginning. Sometimes when we exit the highway, the night sky changes. I've been making a new spreadsheet so we can compare—"

"Yeah, that's what's going to save us from the infinite void. You've cracked it, buddy! All we need is one more fucking spreadsheet," Faye says sardonically.

"Oh, I'm *sorry,* Faye! Is being pissed off about it and doing nothing so much more effective?" Shel claps back. He pauses, and waits for a reaction from the rest of us that doesn't come. We're just so damn tired.

Shel, of course, carries on talking anyway. "Listen, I was thinking of setting up a time-lapse camera in that 151 tower to make some observations the next time we come round to it… when we find it again," he says. "If it's a circle, we'll get back there eventually."

"What if we just turn around?" Faye says. "We just passed the tower a few hours ago. So if we drive the other way, if we backtrack… we should get back there, right?"

I think of what Ramone told Shel, about driving past the gas station on that first night, then doubling back to find it gone, and I shiver.

There's a strange, nauseated feeling in my stomach, like this is all just a bit too familiar. I rack my brain, wondering if someone has mentioned backtracking with the van before. Surely in all this time, one of us has already thought of *driving the other way.* Maybe we've even tried it already. I don't remember us doing it… but I don't exactly *not* remember it either.

Despite Shelton's careful record-keeping, despite all our data and timestamps and *material evidence,* I wonder if we've been in here a lot longer than we think. Time moves oddly here. Sometimes I feel like I've learned and unlearned things, like whole lifetimes of understanding have slipped through my fingers. Maybe it's the *future* I'm feeling somehow, that glimmer of possibility that still lies ahead of us. Maybe the veil is thin in some places, bending the barrier between *wherever we are* and the world we used to inhabit. A world where time moves forward normally. A world where we *live,* if we could only reach it.

) ● (

The next morning, when we re-join the highway, Spencer drives east. I'm pretty sure this direction change is the most overcomplicated endeavor in the history of roadtrips, because first we have to record *everything*—for science, Shelton says. He makes note of it all: the exit number we last left, what was ahead and behind us, how many trees he can see at the horizon line, the position of the sun in the sky, the fucking temperature.

And then we drive. We're going in the opposite direction now, we are, we're sure of it.

Until we *aren't.*

Because eventually, we do come upon a familiar-looking exit again—and I know with sinking certainty that this is the convenience store we've been to twice before. Sure enough, our graffitied names are outside on the table. My five-dollar bill is sitting inside the till. Even that rusty old truck is still parked out back. *Fuck.*

"If we're really backtracking," Ramone says, "then shouldn't we have seen the Exit 151 tower first, way before we got back here? Even if it was a circle—"

"Yeah," says Shel, his voice somewhere between astonished and defeated. "Yeah, definitely. I... I don't think it's a circle. And... I don't think we're backtracking."

Faye looks like she might be hyperventilating. She's leaning against the side of the van, her face even paler than usual, her eyebrows furrowed into the kind of pained expression that I've only seen her make when she's about to barf. I debate about putting my hand on her shoulder, but there's every chance she might actually bite me if I touch her.

"What *are* we doing, then?" Spence asks. There's a trembling sincerity in the question that borders on desperation. He's begging one of us to answer him, even if we have to make something up. Sometimes I think we just need to hear an answer, even if we know damn well it's all bullshit. We need to hear *something* comforting, so we can reassure each other that we're still okay.

Mom always knew what to say when we were scared, always had an explanation when we got confused. But it's not as if any of us has a goddamn clue about anything now. And Mom isn't here to make it up for us.

"We're not backtracking, so... we're... we must be doing something else," Shelton says, sublimely unhelpful. He jabs hard at the bridge of his glasses, staring off into the middle distance. "Yeah. We're... doing... something else."

Suddenly, it occurs to me that the convenience store exit is still on the same side of the highway as it was before. That means we must be going west again, somehow.

Or else we're going nowhere, because we've never really been going anywhere.

We really are right back where we started. *Again.*

That night, we pull over at a campsite we definitely haven't been to before. There's nothing here: no charred outline of an old campfire in the dirt; no stones arranged in the rough circle of a makeshift fire pit. In the past, we've sometimes found the remnants of previous campfires and small woodpiles when we camped for the night. I've found myself wondering who the last people were to have passed through these places, before everyone else vanished. Now, a chill goes through me as I wonder how many of those ghostly remnants of campfires past were actually *our own.*

Wouldn't we have recognized them if they were ours? Or are they the ashes of parts of ourselves that we've already forgotten, things we've burned to dust and kicked dirt over before we drove away from them?

Perhaps they were not so buried after all. Perhaps there are things inside us that we burn down again and again, but we keep coming back to the ashes anyway.

"Look... listen... we still have options," Shel is saying. He's a little bit drunk, slurring his words as he waves one of his notebooks around in the firelight. "Personally... I don't think we've done enough yet with trying to go *sideways.* I mean, going *off the road*, leaving the highway completely. Like... we could leave the van and go on foot, right? Those drones that disappeared... what if they got *out?* Sideways. Yeah. Sideways has to be the answer. We could take the walkie-talkies with us... an' walk as far as they'll reach... an' make a chain, so then we could—"

"No!" Spence shouts loudly, startling everybody. He stands up from his lawn chair so suddenly that he knocks his beer over. It spills into the fire pit, the liquid fizzing away into the embers. "Shel, stop. It's fucking *pointless!* There's no way out of here!"

"Wowwww. Great attitude, big bro," Shel drawls, flashing him a sarcastic thumbs up. "Giving up! That's a fantastic idea. Who's with him?"

"Shelton, shut up. You don't understand."

"What, hmm? What is it that I don't understand?" Shel kicks at Spence's mostly empty beer bottle, making it spin over the dirt. "Do enlighten me, Spencer. I'd *love* to hear some more goddamn sad-ass pessimism."

Spence glances over at Ramone, and there's something nervous in his eyes when he looks at them. His voice drops low. "Ramone," he says. "I think... we need to show everybody what we found."

Ramone gives the smallest of nods. They stand up and walk slowly over to the van. We all wait in silence as they go inside, the four of us staring anxiously at the camper door until they finally come back out with something cradled in their hands.

We watch them walk back toward us like they're carrying some kind of precious magic item. Or a curse. Silently, they hold it out to us on their outstretched palms.

A small drone, exactly like one of Shelton's. And attached to it is a cracked orange phone case, with the logo of a local small-town rugby team on it. The junior league team that Spence coaches every Saturday.

They've got Spence's lost phone.

"When?" Shel asks through clenched teeth. "When did you know about this?"

"A while ago," says Spence, looking away. "Actually... the night after we picked up Ramone. We found it by the trees, behind the campsite." He glances at Ramone, an apology in his eyes. "I asked them not to say anything to anyone else. This is totally on me."

I can't read Shel's expression. Maybe his emotions have just short-circuited or something, leaving his face a grey, stiff mask that's somewhere between incredulous horror and devastated betrayal. He's shaking with rage. "What the *hell* is wrong with you, Spencer? Why would you want to hide something like this?"

"I don't know! I just... I wasn't even really sure what it meant! Besides, there was nothing we could do about it anyway, what was the point of telling you?" Spence protests. "Sometimes maybe it's just easier to pretend something didn't happen than to admit that everything is absolutely fucked. I thought you'd know all about that, *Shelton*, since you're the one who acts like you're so goddamn fine all the time."

Shel looks wounded. "What the fuck, dude. No! *You* said we're supposed to be a team!" he shouts. "What happened to having each other's back? I've been working my ass off, keeping track of the moon, logging what exits we took, making all those notes about gas mileage, when all the while you were just *screwing us over* by hiding crucial data! For what?" His voice is still rising. "Answer me!"

It's been years since I've seen my brothers have an actual screaming fight. Spence *hates* conflict. Even when he's real mad at Shel or me, he hardly ever raises his voice. He usually just curls in on himself, speaks in short sentences, goes quiet, shuts us out. And Shel can be a hothead, but he'll slam doors and blast loud music before he'll ever actually *yell* at anyone.

Both of my brothers are standing up now, standing on opposite sides of the campfire and glaring at each other. I feel Ramone's gaze on me as they turn their head in my direction, probably searching my face for a clue as to whether there's any real chance that they're going to start punching each other. But I don't take my eyes off Spence and Shel.

Spence is holding both of his hands up now, palms facing toward Shel. "Look. Just take a deep breath, Shel. Maybe we should all just chill out, take a minute, and then we can—"

"Fuck *chilling out,*" Shel snaps. "Are you going to answer me or not?" He stalks around to Spence's side of the fire, his fists clenched, and gets right up in Spence's face. "You are so convinced that you need to *control everything* and protect us that you won't let anyone else make a goddamn decision! You've been doing this ever since Mom died!"

"Shel, stop it!" Faye shouts. "Stop acting like such a dick and let's talk about this like adults!" She gets in between the two of them, stretching one arm protectively across Spence's chest, separating my brothers like a safety barrier.

I've literally never seen *any* of them acting like this. The only time I've even seen the trio have anything like a serious disagreement was when they fell out after that awful party. Five years ago, the summer we lost Mom and our world fell apart.

Ramone is standing with one hand pressed to their mouth, still clutching Shel's drone with the other. Their eyes dart from me to my brothers to Faye, then back to me.

"Shel," Faye says again. "Back off."

Spence still doesn't say anything, and so Shel whirls on Faye. "Why the hell are you defending him, Faye? Huh?" He steps toward Ramone and grabs the drone, ripping Spence's phone out of it and throwing the rest of it onto the grass. He shakes the cracked phone at Faye. "Don't you think he should have just told us the truth about this?"

"Yes!" Faye shrieks. "Yes, yes actually, I do! But I also remember having this same goddamn argument with *you* in Marky-O's driveway once, Shelton. The *objective purpose of truth?* Remember that? The Shitshow Saturday?"

"Oh, don't you *dare*, Faye—" Shel starts.

Spence kind of freezes and tilts his head to one side, and his jaw visibly clenches.

"No, I'm saying it, Shel." Faye takes a deep breath. "I was going to take it to my goddamn grave... but I don't care anymore. If we're all stuck here, if we're trapped forever, then we might as well all be dead *anyway!*"

"Faye," Shel starts, his face almost pleading. "*Don't.*"

"That night at Marky-O's party...the Shitshow Saturday..." Faye says, turning toward Spencer. "Shel and I slept together." The words run out of her mouth all at once, as if she needs to say it as fast as possible. "Shel *wasn't* passed out drunk in the basement when you and Stacey were looking for him. He was with me, in the pool house. And I know, *I know*, we all had the pact that we would *never*, and... I felt fucking terrible about it." She looks at the ground, averting her eyes from Spence's. "And yes, Shel and I both knew damn well that *you* had feelings for me back then. But the thing is, I'd just broken up with Sabrina, and she quit the studio, and then my car was broken into... shit was just *so* messed up that summer. And Shel was upset about your mom and everything, and... we just...we kind of...we..."

Spence is standing there with a pained grimace on his face, pressing his fingers to his temples. I feel like we're all moving in slow motion, as if a bullet has just been fired and it's suspended in mid-air between us, waiting for Spence to either Matrix-dodge it or collapse and shatter like glass.

"Faye... I've known exactly what went down at that party ever since the night it happened," Spence says slowly.

Faye turns to Shel with a sharp, incredulous intake of breath. "What? You *told* him? After all that bullshit?"

"No." Spence is shaking his head, holding up his hand. "No. Shel never told me anything. But I saw your location, Faye. We all had each other on that Find Friends app! When I was trying to call you and you weren't answering, I checked it—and I could see damn well that you were at Marky-O's. And so was Shel. His phone was still on." He drags his gaze to Shel, and he looks more exasperated than angry. In fact, he almost laughs. "Guess you didn't throw your phone in the pool till after. Genius."

Shel opens his mouth as if he's going to say something, then slowly closes it again like he's thought better of it.

"I wanted to tell you, Spencer," Faye says. "Honestly. I did want to. But Shel said there was no point. We were arguing about it in the car for like two hours." She's still got one arm up like she's separating my brothers. "But... *I* was the one who fucked up the pact, Spence. It was me, it was totally my bad. You guys were grieving, and Shel was a complete mess. He was drunk, and sad, and I shouldn't have—"

"Faye, would you shut up already with all that martyr stuff?" Shel interrupts. "Bad judgment, bad timing, yadda yadda, whatever. It's not like you mind-controlled me or something! You just fucking *kissed* me! Everything from there on out was on both of us. And I wasn't even that drunk, I was just giving myself an excuse!" He takes a deep breath. "Look... I didn't give a damn about anyone except myself that summer. I slept with you because I think I *wanted* to mess shit up. I *wanted* you to get pissed off at me, and stop caring about me, and I just wanted to destroy everything, because *nothing* had any goddamn point!"

There are tears pooling in the corners of Faye's eyes now, smudging her knife-sharp eyeliner. I can probably count on one hand the number of times I've ever seen Faye cry, and two of them were when I was a kid.

Finally, Shel throws his hands up, glaring at Spence and then Faye. "Fine, you got me. I said what I said. *What is the objective purpose of telling the truth when there's nothing you can do about it*? So I guess you were right. Are you happy now?"

Ramone is looking away from all of us now, pointedly averting their eyes, like they know this is Kells business and they want to give us some privacy. They're with us, but they're not one of us.

Not that we're doing a great job of being 'us.' The Kells family is fracturing around me, like it's the Shitshow Saturday all over again.

"Shelton, you are *such* an asshole." The rage flares in Faye's eyes again. "You know what, fuck you. And fuck you, too, Spence. In five years you never thought to tell me that *you already knew*?"

She spins around abruptly and starts to walk away.

"Faye! Don't—" Spence starts.

Faye turns around and flips two middle fingers up, one aimed toward each of my brothers. Then she stalks back to the camper van, goes inside, and slams the door.

Shel makes to follow her, but Spence grabs his wrist and holds him back with a fierce glare. And Shel, surprisingly, lowers his eyes and relents. My brothers walk off together and go talk around the other side of the camper, out of our view. I can hear their low, tense voices, but I can't make out what they're saying. At least they aren't yelling anymore.

Ramone sits back down on one of the lawn chairs. They fish a rolled joint out of their pocket and light it up with a long sigh. They hold it out and offer it to me, but I wave it away.

We just sit there in silence for a while, looking at the fire, and I wonder if they're straining to hear what the guys are talking about behind the camper, just like I am. But I can't overhear a damn thing.

Eventually, I see my brothers come back around the van. They both knock on the side door, and they stand there for a long time in the dark, shoulder to shoulder, waiting for Faye to come to the door. And then, at last, a wedge of light pours out of the doorway as Faye finally opens it. With her standing on the raised ledge of the camper, they're all exactly the same height.

Now it's the three of them standing there, my brothers facing Faye, all of them talking to each other. I hear her voice, softly, but I still can't tell what any of them are saying. And then, Faye steps aside, and my brothers both walk into the camper, closing the door behind them.

Ramone and I sit, and we wait. Ramone looks at me anxiously, their gaze a question. *This is* your *family drama,* their eyes say. *How bad is it?*

"They're the eternal trio. Indestructible," I say, blinking back tears. "They'll be all right. I know it."

I've unconsciously pulled that vending machine quarter out of my pocket, and I'm spinning it round and round on my palm. I sink back in my chair, watching firelight glinting from its unusually reflective surface.

"And what about *you*, Stacey?" Ramone asks.

"Me, too," I tell them. "We're the Kells family. We always manage to pull it together in the end. Have each other's backs, no matter what." I smile at them, letting a tear slip down my cheek. "I think you fit right in."

We sit in quiet companionship for a while more, watching the waning fire. Then finally, Ramone puts out their joint, and I pocket the shiny quarter again. We kick dirt over the embers in the fire pit and we fold up the lawn chairs.

And we make our way slowly back to the camper to rejoin the others.

) ● (

The calico cat jumps out of the bushes as I'm exiting the gas station bathroom. I slide the plastic keychain into my pocket as I watch the cat duck under our van and scamper to the other side, where it runs away between the gas pumps.

I walk right past the argument at the vending machine, and I keep walking out onto the parking lot, still watching the cat as it weaves its way swiftly around the pumps. But they aren't gas pumps anymore— no, suddenly this is a games arcade, and the pumps are a row of old-school arcade machines, stretching as far as I can see.

It's that weird endless arcade inside the Sunnyview Motel.

I follow the cat further and further as it delves deeper into the shadows. Every so often it looks back, like it's waiting for me to catch up, until it stops in the place where I saw it before— right in front of the yellow jukebox. MEGA-MEGA-HITS.

I take out my Sharpie and I start to write on the glass that covers the song selection screen: *Stacey M. Kells was here, Stacey M. Kells was here again, Stacey M. Kells is alive, Stacey M. Kells exists—*

Somewhere behind me, the thick platform of Faye's boot makes contact with the vending machine outside the Legend Roadstop and hits the metal with a reverberating clang. It sounds exactly like that blue door hitting the trash can at the Exit 151 tower.

And as I wake up, I hear the faint tinkle of a single shiny quarter coming back in the coin return.

) ● (

Soft daylight is streaming into my eyes as I rub them with my palms, momentarily disoriented by being in two places at once, until I realize I'm on my cot at the back of the camper. Ramone and Spencer are both asleep on Faye's cot nearby, squished into the small space together.

Ramone is propped up with their head resting against the wall underneath the digital clock—it's 6:02 in the morning, somewhere—and Spence is lying across their lap, their arms locked around him to keep him from falling onto the floor.

I tiptoe out of bed and I stick my head through the bead curtain into Shel's office. Shel's passed out in his sleeping bag underneath the desk, but there's no sign of Faye. I check the front bench, and she's not in there either.

I open the side door as quietly as I can, and I slip out of the camper into the early morning light. I let out a breath of relief when I see that Faye's there—she's sitting on the grass next to the remains of last night's fire, drawing something in her sketchbook.

I approach quietly, crouching down next to her. "Hey."

"Hey," she whispers, turning to me.

She hasn't got any makeup on, and her eyes are still slightly red-rimmed after last night. But her face has that angelic, delicate look that she usually only gets when she's sleeping, and I realize it's because she looks...*peaceful.*

"Everything okay?" I ask her hopefully.

"Yeah. Probably. It will be." She gives a tired half-smile, and I wonder if she went to sleep last night at all. "Always is, eventually."

I look at the sketchbook that's lying open across her knees. "What're you working on, another tattoo design? Can I see?"

She tilts the page toward me. It's a calico cat, drawn long and sinewy like it's mid-run. Its tail is a fluid, wavy line streaming behind it, its legs outstretched, and it's leaping past a round full moon, surrounded by lines of constellations.

"I'm not done yet, but I think it's getting there," Faye says. "It's that cat we saw back in the arcade. The image of it has weirdly just kind of been... stuck in my head."

I stare at the page, my heart skipping a little at the sight of it. And when I look up again and look back toward the camper, I see a flicker of movement from the corner of my eye.

At first, I think that one of the others got up, that maybe I saw a curtain move, or else somebody's about to come out of the van. But no—whatever moved was lower to the ground, beside the front wheel.

There's something down there. A *cat,* just slipping out of view under the camper.

I leap to my feet. "Holy shit! Do you see it, Faye?"

Her head snaps up. "See what?"

I don't wait for her reaction. I scramble over there, rushing breathlessly to the other side of the van to see where it's gone.

I get there just in time to see it take off at speed into the trees.

I don't think, I don't stop, I just follow it. I have to see.

I *run*.

I race headlong into the small patch of trees behind our campsite, ignoring Faye shouting after me that I didn't take a walkie-talkie. I run faster and faster, my feet flying over moss and dirt and rocks and tree roots, like I haven't run since I last did a school cross-country day. My lungs burn with exertion, my breath coming in short, halting gasps, but I don't pause. I run and run and run, following the calico cat.

There's a terror in it, and a freedom too—I haven't truly been alone since we've been here. I can't stop myself from looking. I want to see where that cat is going. I *need* to see.

I crest the last little bit of the incline, where the path through the trees ahead of me turns sharply to the left and begins to tilt downward. I'm standing at the very top of a cliff, an outcropping that overlooks a highway.

The cat has scampered off somewhere, I can't see it anymore.

But I see where I am. I'm looking over the quarry, looking down from the top of *that* cliff. Below me is the dead end of Exit 151, with its strange control tower and the gravel parking area and those orange cones delineating the entrance.

Except that all of the cones here are still standing up, and I can see yellow caution tape flapping from the arch in front of the tower doorway. Of course, it *could* be a different tower, but...

I squint into the sun, wishing that somehow I had thought to bring the binoculars. There's a small, dark-haired figure in the distance, just walking up to the tower from the side of the road.

It hits me then: the highway is down there—*our* highway. The same highway that's somewhere behind me is also far below me; it's all around us. It winds through everything we ever see.

I watch the figure pause to look up at the tower before they approach it, probably wondering what the hell it is, just like we did the first time we saw it. If they looked slightly to the left and up to the ridge, we'd be looking right at each other.

They're much too far away for me to see their face clearly... but that puffy, bright purple jacket is unmistakable. There's no doubt it's them.

Ramone. Ramone, arriving at the tower.

I watch them walking across the graveled area. They rip down the yellow caution tape, bunch it up, and throw it on the ground. And then, one by one, they kick over all the cones from one side of the entry, scattering them across the gravel with all the indifference of someone who's been wandering an empty world alone for a week. They walk up to the metal door at the base of the tower, stopping to adjust the camping backpack on their shoulder. Then they disappear from my sight as they open the door and go inside.

My heart is pounding in my throat, beating with the certainty of what my mind can't comprehend. And then I look over to my right, where instead of a sheer drop, the hill slopes downward much more gently. Below me is a wide stretch of open desert... and there, further down, is a pink brick building with a pool on one side. *The back of the Sunnyview Motel.*

I can just see the side of the building, and from this angle I can see the pool deck, but not the covered part of the patio or the motel rooms or the front door.

I can see the empty expanse of the vacant parking lot beside the motel. There's exactly one vehicle there, parked sideways across several spots.

Ours.

Our weird little camper van, with the red and yellow stripes Spence painted down the sides and the satellite dish Shel mounted on the roof, is parked next to the Sunnyview Motel.

I descend the slope carefully, bracing my feet against rocks and roots, until I'm down on the flat expanse of terrain at the bottom of the hill. My heart thunders in my chest, and I'm breathing in short, painful gasps.

My brain rebels. *No no no no.* This isn't possible.

I end up near the path that goes around the back of the building, in pretty much the exact same place where Faye and I were walking when we found that open window. The window is there, but it's closed, sealed tight. I try unsuccessfully to pry my fingers into the gap around it. I can't budge it, nor can I see through it to the arcade beyond.

I keep looking behind me, terrified of who I might see, but there's nobody in sight. We must all be inside the motel somewhere. Maybe Faye and I are exploring that multitude of labyrinthine hallways. Ramone and my brothers might be upstairs around the other side, searching one of the motel rooms. But we're *here*, somewhere.

We. My brothers, Faye, Ramone, *myself*—some past or future version of us, of our van, of our stuff, is here. All of it exists at once.

I'm *here*, and I'm also inside the motel. Ramone is inside the motel, but also just arriving at the tower. And all of them are back *there* with the van, too, at the campsite I just left.

Part of me wants to run around to the parking lot and go look in the camper van, and I'm about to do it when I suddenly notice something. A flash of movement on the flimsy metal fire escape that's just beyond the pool. That calico cat, whisking its tail back and forth as it circles on the landing. I move closer.

And then I see it: there's a *door* back here, tucked out of sight. A piece of tattered tarpaulin hangs from the fire escape stairs in front of it, so it doesn't look like anything much from a distance. But when I lift the tarp aside, there's a bright pink door behind it.

And there's a key on a plastic keyring hanging in the door. It looks just like all the motel room keys: a yellow sun logo with MAINTENANCE printed on it instead of a room number.

I turn the key and fling the door open, and I already know exactly what I'll find beyond it. It leads into the game room, the *arcade*. The same infinite, cavernous room that I climbed into through that window.

The same one I saw again in my dream.

The cat is here, weaving between my legs. It jumps through the door ahead of me and I follow it into the arcade, still clutching that maintenance key in my hand.

Inside, I hurry past the game machines and go over to the narrow window that faces out onto the pool side. There's only a single window in here—this has to be it. I manage to heave it open a crack, and it sticks at first, but then it slides the rest of the way up. I poke my head out cautiously, and I can't see or hear anybody outside... but it's now or never.

I don't know if I dare. I don't know if I *should*. But I have to know. I have to *see*.

I fish in my pocket for the shiny quarter that I've been holding on to ever since Faye kicked that vending machine at the Legend Roadstop. My vision blurs as I run further back into the room.

I lean dizzily against the yellow jukebox—MEGA-MEGA-HITS— and I push the coin into the slot on the machine. *Clink, clink, clink.* The quarter falls down, the eerie sound echoing through the room like a bell tolling the end of all things.

A number '1' appears in the little LED window at the top. One credit.

I scroll through the songs with shaking hands and make my selection. The jukebox clicks, engaging the track as I hold myself steady against the machine, my palms flat on the little display, my knees quaking.

The song starts to play, the volume low, but conspicuous in the motel's silence.

Nothing happens.

Nothing happens.

Nothing happens.

And then, I hear a sound like scattering pebbles, little pieces of concrete hitting the wall outside. I hear the scuff of a boot, then another little shower of rocks.

And Faye's voice: "Shhh, shhh! Stop, Stace, listen! D'you hear that?" A pause. "God*damn* it, I *hate* this fucking song!"

Somehow, I find my footing. I look down that long, endless row of game machines, the cavernous expanse of the arcade ready to consume me.

And I run back to the maintenance door.

I clutch the key, and I run with my eyes half shut, fumbling for the door handle as I fling it outward with all the wild terror of someone running for their life.

) ● (

I half-stumble, half-fall through the doorway and out into a convenience store parking lot. Behind me is a heavily graffitied metal door, and the air has that faint waft of stale pee, cleaning products, and cheap pink hand soap.

I look down at the key I'm clutching in my hand—it's the grubby, worn plastic keyring with the key to the gas station bathroom. In faded black Sharpie, it says *WC Legend Roadstop.*

A calico cat hops out of the bushes, and weaves around my feet once before it scampers off in the direction of our parked camper.

My brothers and Faye are there, gathered in the glow of the vending machine.

"Ah, dammit. I think it ate one of our quarters!" Faye is saying as she crouches by the coin return.

"It's broken," Spencer sighs. "Look here. Says *ERROR.*" He looks at Faye. "How about I just go back and buy you a Dr Pepper inside?"

Shel looks like he's about to say something, a strange expression crossing his face as he reaches for the vending machine button. Then he pulls his hand back.

"Nah, wait—*I'll* go get it," he says. "C'mon. Give that here." He holds out his hand and takes the remaining change from Faye, then walks off to the convenience store entrance.

Faye and Spence blink at each other for a moment, then look away again. They stay standing there, staring at the vending machine and then looking back at each other, both lost in thought. They don't see me walk up to them.

"Do you ever just... feel like you've *been* somewhere before?" Spence says.

"Oh, yeah, déjà vu. For sure. Majorly." Faye's forehead furrows. "It's these roadside stops, man, they're all the same. Liminal places, you know? On the edge of things, like... if there's some kind of veil, we're *this close* to it. These places do weird things to your brain."

"Yeah. An' our brains are pretty damn weird already," Spence laughs. He sighs, pauses. "Goddammit. I've just been so damn stressed, Faye. I'm sorry if I... y'know... I'm sorry for what I said... about letting you drive. I was just—"

"S'okay." She elbows him gently. "I know it's tomorrow, Spence. Five years, since your mom. I get it."

He scuffs his feet. "Maybe we should do something."

"Yeah," Faye says, her voice soft. "You should *live*."

I reach out then and I take Spencer's hand, and he turns to look at me like he's seeing me for the first time. "Oh! Hey, kiddo. What's up? You good?"

"Yeah." I squeeze his hand. "I think I'm good."

We stand there in a little circle until Shel comes back with the Dr Pepper, and he presses it into Faye's hand like some kind of peace offering. He looks around at us, and then for some reason I can't fathom, my emotionally constipated brother raises his fist, like he's gonna do one of those cheesy team fist-bump things.

I want to laugh—we're not exactly the kind of group that has a funny team move or a secret handshake or something. But... maybe we really are roadtrip-bonding. Maybe liminal places really *do* make weird things happen to your brain.

Spence sticks his fist out too, then Faye, and then me, and we bump our knuckles together, smiling at each other.

Then Spence spins the keys to the camper around on his finger and casually flicks them over to Faye. She's so surprised that she barely catches them, but there's real joy on her face.

When I look back at the gas pumps, I see that somebody is walking toward us from the direction of the highway.

There's something familiar about them, but I don't think I've ever seen them before. They're probably about the same age as us, twenty-something, with light brown skin, spiky hair and *the* most perfectly arched jet-black eyebrows I've ever seen. They've got a bright purple jacket tied around their waist, and a big camping backpack on.

"'Scuse me?" they say as they come up to our little huddle.

Spencer turns around, and for a second I see his eyes widen, like he might've thought he recognized them, too. "Hey," he says with a goofy smile.

"Sorry to bother you, but... could I possibly use your phone?" They hold up a mobile phone and shake it. "I've got no signal, and my car just broke down over there. I need to call for a tow."

Spence reaches into his pocket and pulls out his phone. He's got the world's ugliest orange phone case, but it's got the logo of the junior league rugby team he coaches on it, and my brother's sentimental like that. He goes to unlock the screen, then frowns.

"Oh, damn," he says. "Looks like I've got no signal either. We must be in a dead zone."

"There's a payphone over there, if it works," Shel says, pointing over by the gas pumps.

Faye snorts. "Damn, I didn't even know those still existed!"

I take a step forward then, and I don't know what possesses me, but I *kick* the vending machine, right in the middle of the metal panel at the base. There's a deep dent there, like several other people have had the same idea already.

My family looks at me in stunned surprise, but I'm immediately vindicated—a single quarter tinkles down into the return, and I retrieve it with a triumphant smile. It's as shiny and new as if no one has ever touched it before.

"Here," I say, holding it out to our new friend. "See if it works."

"Thanks, mate!" They take the coin gratefully, and I admire their glittery neon manicure. They've got tiny silver moon phases stenciled on each nail. "It'd damn well better work, because everything has well and truly fucked up tonight," they laugh.

"Not everything," Spencer says. He's smiling like I haven't seen him smile in a long time.

We all walk together to the payphone, and I catch one last glimpse of that calico cat, disappearing into the shadows beyond the gas pumps.

Not everything means something. But my name is Stacey M. Kells, and I exist.

ACKNOWLEDGMENTS

An immense thank you to my wonderful editors Jendia Gammon and Gareth L. Powell. You both understood this weird little book so deeply, and it's been a joy to be part of your launch year at Stars and Sabers!

To my incredible literary agent, Ernie Chiara: thank you so much for your support, your advice and your unparalleled enthusiasm. You have changed my journey in innumerable ways.

Thanks also to Scarlett R. Algee for a keen eye on the line edits, and to Kim Herbst for the care and imagination that went into creating the stunning cover artwork!

To my crit partners, beta readers, and friends all over the creative community: you are amazing. Thank you for inspiring and uplifting me. Special thanks goes out to the earliest readers of this story: Monica, Rebecca, Kate M, Claire, Khan, Harry, Kate P, Kerbie and Meredith.

To my family, born and chosen: my eternal thanks for your encouragement and your relentless cheerleading in every one of my endeavors. You have been a light in the labyrinth.

And to M, my love and most heartfelt gratitude, always.

Not everything means something, but some things mean the world.

ABOUT THE AUTHOR

Ren Hutchings is a speculative fiction writer, writing mentor, editor, and lifelong SFF fan. She loves pop science, unexplained mysteries, 90s music, collecting outdated electronics, and pondering about alternate universes. Most of what she writes involves space, time, history, and/or uncanny liminal places. Ren is the author of twisty sci-fi books including *Under Fortunate Stars* and *An Unbreakable World* (Solaris Books) and *The Legend Liminal* (Stars and Sabers), as well as short fiction. You can find Ren online at renhutchings.com, and on social media as @voidcricket.